THE RIVER RUN

The Legend of Big Heart · Book 3

Alfreda Beartrack-Algeo

7th GENERATION
Summertown, Tennessee

Library of Congress Cataloging-in-Publication Data available upon request.

This is a work of historical fiction. All incidents, events, dialogue, names, and characters except for some well-known historical figures are products of the author's imagination and are not to be construed as real. Where real-life historical figures appear, the situations, incidents, and dialogues concerning those persons are fictional and are not intended to depict actual events. In all other respects, any likeness to actual persons, living or dead, or actual events is purely coincidental.

Cover and interior design: John Wincek

7th Generation
Book Publishing Company
PO Box 99
Summertown, TN 38483
888-260-8458
bookpubco.com
nativevoicesbooks.com

ISBN: 978-1-57067-413-6
E-book ISBN: 978-1-57067-803-5

29 28 27 26 25 24   1 2 3 4 5 6 7 8 9

CONTENTS

1   World Upside Down 1

2   New Rules 7

3   The New School 15

4   A New Reality 19

5   Eyes Looking Back 25

6   Good to Be Home 31

7   Grandfather's Journey
and Our Return 39

8   Things Are About to Change 47

9   On the Run 55

10   Hitchhiking 61

11   Sioux City or Bust 69

12   Carnival World 77

13   Object of Wonder 91

14   Rumor Has It   97

15   The Letter 103

16   Let the Thunder Begin 115

17   Cry Victory 121

18   Last of Her Kind 131

19   Gangsters on the Run 137

20   Real Water, Real Me 143

Afterword 153
The Pick-Sloan Act and
the Five Giant Beavers

About the Author 155

World Upside Down

October came on with splashes of yellow and orange. It was the first moon of winter 1931 and the day that my world turned upside down. It started out like any other Monday "read-a-thon" at Iron Nation Day School. We all looked forward to the reading event and the treat our teacher, Mrs. Red Elk, would bring us: her famous peanut brittle. In all our excitement, no one could imagine how the day would end.

Some of my younger classmates brought stuffed animals to our event to use as props. Jerry and Jamie Bull Elk even brought their pet mice, Johnny and Timmy, in a cardboard shoebox. They said the mice would add to their story, *The Tale of Johnny Town-Mouse* by Beatrix Potter. Mrs. Red Elk made sure the shoebox lid was closed and put the mice on a shelf behind the door. They were creating quite a stir with the girls.

My friend Sage and I were taking turns reading out loud from *The Velveteen Rabbit* by Margery Williams. I felt silly, but it was one of Sage's favorite childhood stories. Besides, I knew the younger students would enjoy it. Sage held a raggedy stuffed rabbit that had one of its red button eyes missing, and I was wearing a black stovepipe hat. I could tell Mrs. Red Elk was pleased with our presentation by the encouraging nods she was giving us.

Whew, the end! We took a bow following a loud round of applause from the class. I couldn't wait to sit down before Mrs. Red Elk started picking on me. *It never failed.*

Mrs. Red Elk said, "That was wonderful. Thank you both. Now, Alfred, can you share with the class one of the lessons *The Velveteen Rabbit* teaches us?"

I muttered, "Ummmm . . . um."

I desperately scanned the faces of my classmates for some help. *Lilly? Beatrice? Margaret? Todd? Tim? . . . Nothing? Darn!* Even my best friends, Orson and Junior, were no help. *Shucks!* They wouldn't make eye contact with me. I was on my own.

Sage came to my rescue. "May I answer for Alfred?"

Whew! Just in time. Sage always knew when I was in a bind. It was like we had an invisible connection.

Mrs. Red Elk said, "Okay, Sage, help Alfred out and tell us what lesson you see in the story of *The Velveteen Rabbit*."

Sage said, "I think the story teaches us that we need to trust others even if we might get hurt. Because deep inside, everybody wants to be liked and loved and wanted and needed. Some days are sad, and some are happy, but that is what makes life real. And maybe that is what makes us real too."

I felt my face turning red. I knew Sage was talking to me. She knew that I was afraid of being hurt and didn't trust anyone, especially adults. Now everybody in the room knew it too.

Thump! Crash! The heavy wooden door of the schoolhouse slammed open and hit the back wall, and three men stormed in. I recognized the dark blue uniforms. They were the Indian police from the Office of Indian Affairs. Sage and I quickly took our seats.

The shoebox flew off the shelf from the force of the door. *Whoa!* Two elated mice scurried across the floor right toward us. The room was in utter chaos. Everyone, including me, pulled our feet up while the Indian police looked on in confusion.

The mice disappeared into the woodpile stacked near the woodstove at the back of the classroom.

Mrs. Red Elk said to the class, "Students, please calm down and stay in your seats."

We all sat at our desks and silently stared at the police officers, wondering what was going to happen next.

Turning to the officers, Mrs. Red Elk said, "May I help you?"

One of the police officers stepped forward. He looked like he was the police captain. "No, you have not done anything wrong. We are here on orders to board up this school. You need to take your students and leave the school grounds immediately."

Mrs. Red Elk asked, "On whose orders?"

The police officer said, "The Office of Indian Affairs of the United States government has proclaimed this order!"

The officers ordered us into the front parking area on the other side of the fence. I felt like a captured animal being prepared for slaughter.

I fidgeted from one foot to the other, not knowing what to expect.

Two police officers with an armful of boards, nails, and a hammer walked toward the front door of the schoolhouse but stopped abruptly in surprise. Mrs. Red Elk stood with outstretched arms, blocking the schoolhouse door.

She said, "I will not leave! This is unlawful! The children have a right to a decent education like any other child in this country."

The officer carrying the hammer dropped it on the ground and grabbed Mrs. Red Elk.

Horrified, we watched in shock as Mrs. Red Elk scuffled with the officer. Her courageous attempt was short-lived. Within seconds the officer had her pinned to the ground.

Sage, still holding the stuffed rabbit, screamed, "Alfred! Please stop them! Please, don't let them hurt my aunt!"

Jerry and Jamie Bull Elk were just as upset. "Alfred, could you please go get our pet mice for us? They might get hurt. Please?"

I felt helpless. My feet wouldn't move; they felt like two lead anvils.

Mrs. Red Elk stood up and brushed herself off. Limping and bruised, she joined us on the other side of the front gate.

I thought, *How did everything change from calm to chaos in a split second? Is this an example of the lesson Sage described from the story of* The Velveteen Rabbit—*that life can be both painful and beautiful at the same time?*

A lone stuffed rabbit lay in the dirt beneath the flagpole. Above, the United States flag whipped and snapped in the breeze. I thought, *This is the same flag that we pledge our allegiance to at the beginning of every school day. "Home of the free and land of the brave." Yes, we might be brave, but as Lakota people, we sure are not free.*

"What is going on here?" It was my grandfather, Thomas Plenty Buffalo. Grandfather was part of a crowd of concerned community members and parents who had gathered around us in the school parking area.

The police captain made certain to keep his distance from the crowd. He stepped up on the bumper of his dusty government car and waved a sheet of paper in the air. "This policy I hold in my hand is from the United States government. It states that all Native American students of school age need to be attending a school approved by the secretary of the Office of Indian Affairs. Whereas Iron Nation Day School does not meet the secretary's criteria, from this day forth, the school will remain closed."

A low murmur spread through the crowd.

Grandfather asked, "Sir, what criteria are you referring to?"

The police captain said, "You will need to take the details up with Superintendent Wright. All we know is that we are here to deliver the papers and board the school up. You have a week to get your children in a government-approved school or face the consequences."

New Rules

The police captain handed the paper down to Grandfather. "Here is a list of approved schools. You all have a good day. Best we get back to the agency before sundown."

The police officers drove away in their cars, leaving a trail of dust. As soon as the dust cleared from the last government car driving down the hill, the crowd erupted in a frenzy.

Without a minute to spare, my grandfather stepped up into the box of his wagon to address the crowd. "Take heed, my relatives! It is important to stay calm and go along with the policy. At least for now. Believe me, we will get to the bottom of this."

"Thomas, what Indian policy are they referring to?" said Harvey Two Crow.

Grandfather answered, "*Kill the Indian, Save the Man* policy, Harvey. Heck, it's the same policy that sent your two younger brothers out east to Carlisle Indian Industrial School in Pennsylvania to learn the white man's ways. If I remember right, only one returned and the other one stayed behind, buried deep in the school cemetery."

Harvey Two Crow lowered his head and nodded sadly.

Mrs. Red Elk was next. "All this is an all-out effort to eradicate our cultural identities, our languages, and our traditions. But I say, policy or not, we find justice!"

"HOKA!" the crowd roared in agreement.

Grandfather stepped down from the back of his wagon. "We will meet at the community center here in Iron Nation on Saturday morning to further discuss this issue."

Reluctantly, the angry crowd thinned out.

The fall evening air was brisk and the shadows long. My younger brother, Elmer, and I sat with our parents and grandparents on my grandparents' front porch. Their log cabin was a short distance from our dingy, windswept two-story house, weathered by the blowing dust and swarms of grasshoppers that battered everything in sight.

Although my parents whispered in muffled voices, we could hear every word they said.

Mother whispered, "Elmer, you are a true rolling stone! You are never satisfied with being in one place for too long. What about our sons? Do we take them with us?"

My grandparents looked straight ahead and pretended they could not hear my parents arguing.

I hugged my yellow Labrador, Chepa, close, more so for comfort than warmth. His warm tongue licked my hand to let me know he loved me no matter what. I already knew I wasn't going to like what my parents were going to say.

Oddly enough, my parents spoke to Elmer and me in monotonous voices, like they'd memorized their lines.

My mother said, "Son, your father and I discussed this situation, and we have decided that it would be best for the both of you to finish out your school year at St. John's Indian School in Chamberlain. Your father thinks this will be a good opportunity for you and your brother to get a good and proper education. As I have told you both over and over, the world is rapidly changing, and we as Native people must change with it to survive."

My father continued where my mother left off. He looked directly at me. "Son, I am sure you will have access to more art scholarships. Maybe even make some new friends. Besides, it's close, and your grandparents could visit you both during the school year. So, what do you think?"

I said, "No! I don't want to go to a different school and leave my friends. And why did you say our grandparents will visit us? What about the both of you? Are you planning on leaving us again?" I glared at my father.

Mother said with a sigh, "Your father just informed me that he has received a wonderful offer from a service buddy in Sioux City, Iowa, for a well-paying job. I know you might not understand, but there is a great depression going on everywhere in the country, and jobs are hard to find. Your father is fortunate to have an opportunity to work."

Smiling, my mother leaned toward me. "Plus, we'll be back home by your birthday on May twenty-fourth, and we will do something fun."

Elmer perked up. "Mama and Papa, I'll go. I'm not afraid."

By the look on my grandparents' faces, they disagreed with my parents' decision, yet they stayed silent.

I knew I couldn't win on this one. I said, "I'll go only if my friends Orson and Junior can go to St. John's too."

My mother said, "We will see what we can do."

Standing up, my father yawned and said to my grandparents, "Thomas and Lucille, thank you for supper, but it's getting late, and we need to get these boys home."

We walked up the dirt road, my father with Elmer and me with my mother. Mother slowed her pace so we could talk.

She said, "Son, I know you don't understand your father at times, but he means well. He has been through unspeakable trauma. We were newly married and I was pregnant with you when your father enlisted in the service. Like most of our Lakota men, he was willing to go fight a war for a country that denied our people citizenship, because to him, it was about protecting not only the people but our sacred lands and water. He was wounded during the Second Battle of the Somme in France while saving the lives of two of his comrades. He was honorably discharged and spent a few months in a military hospital recovering. When he returned home, he wasn't the same man who left us."

We finally reached our front yard. *Whew!* I thought. I was still upset about the decision to send me away, and the last thing I wanted to hear was my parents' life stories.

My mother stopped and turned toward me. I thought, *Oh no, now what is she going to say?*

My mother said, "Son, please forgive your father for sending you away and not being there for you when you needed him most. He loves you beyond measure. Please understand that your father's wounds go far deeper than the scars on his body. The war swallowed part of his soul, and no ceremony can bring it back. This is what we have, and we just must accept it. Understand?"

I said, "Yes, Mother, I understand, and I will go along with your decision just for you."

The next day I was still bothered by my conversation with my mother when my friends Orson, Junior, Elizabeth, and Sage stopped by to see me. It was just what I needed.

I said to them, "Follow me. We need to talk!" I pointed toward Medicine Creek and my special hideaway. We reached the giant cottonwood tree that was hidden in the thicket along the banks of the creek. We seated ourselves in a circle beneath the tree. I grabbed a dried branch from the ground to use as a talking staff.

Junior was first to go. "My grandmother is putting me in St. John's Indian School, and I don't want to go."

Orson was next. "That's where I'm going too."

Sage received the makeshift staff. She said, "Elizabeth and I are going to Pierre Indian School because that is where my aunt got a job teaching."

Sage handed over the staff, and all eyes were on me. I said, "Elmer and I will be going to St. John's too." I tried to make light of our dilemma. "I guess we will have good stories to tell each other next summer."

Sage leaned over and kissed me on the cheek. "You bet we will!"

The breeze rustled far above, showering us with dried gold and brown leaves. My spirit rock pressed hot against my chest, and I knew life would never be the same again.

"Time for fun," I said. We all laughed and played a stick game the rest of the afternoon. My thoughts lingered on how soft Sage's lips had felt, which helped get my mind off the dreadful feeling I had inside. *Hmmm.*

The New School

The bleak barrack-style compound sat isolated a few miles north of the town of Chamberlain. A sign posted above the main door at St. John's Indian School read: Anyone Caught Speaking Lakota or Practicing Any Semblance of a Ceremony Will Be Severely Disciplined.

It was the first day at school, and I learned quickly what happened when you forgot to follow the rules.

"*Hihanni waste* (good morning), Sister Rachel. How are you today?"

I hardly had time to see the wooden stick before it met my face. *WHACK! WHACK! WHACK! WHACK!* Sister Rachel then hit my back with her wooden walking stick, causing more pain. She even left an imprint of her stick on my back.

Sister Rachel was a frightful sight. Her thin, pale face was pulled back tight by the black hat and veil that surrounded it. This black costume

15

the women wore was called a habit. Her iron-gray eyes looked extra large and extra mean behind her thick-rimmed spectacles, and her stern mouth was puckered up in anger.

She looked scary, but it was her hard breathing that alarmed me most. Sister Rachel shouted, "Get up, young man! Come with me now!"

I followed her as she hobbled down a long corridor and down cement steps to a cellar. I wondered what was next. With one heave, she shoved me through the cellar door.

Sister Rachel hissed, "I will not stand for any of your heathen ways, young man! You will stay here in the repentance cellar until you repent for your disobedience and are ready to follow the rules!"

The thick cellar door slammed shut. The silence swallowed up her retreating footsteps, and I was alone in the cold, dark cellar. Feelings of abandonment and insignificance cut through me like broken glass. What did she mean by repent? What had I done wrong?

I screamed into the empty darkness: "Mother! Father! You lied to me! Where are you now?"

I fought against it with all my might, but a tear rose from deep inside me. All my pain, my fear, and my anger were bound onto that one tear. It trickled down my cheek, onto my shoulder, and down my arm, then dripped onto the hard dirt-packed floor. A blue spirit light appeared where my tear soaked into the dirt. The small space lit up with an iridescent blue hue, and air fanned against my wet face. A swooshing noise filled the cellar.

Whoooosh. Flap. My spirit helper, the golden eagle, was here to offer me his strength. In a matter of seconds, the room filled with flashing blue spirit lights. Another swooshing sound, and my spirit helper disappeared into the thin, chilly air. The blue lights faded and followed him back to the other side.

I felt stronger and more determined. I decided I would never allow anyone to ever make me cry again, no matter how much I was hurt.

A New Reality

Maybe it was one day, or maybe it was two. I can't exactly remember.

CLICK! Creaaaak. The heavy cellar door squeaked open. Rushing air filled the space, and I could faintly make out a tall shadow filling the doorway.

The shadow said, "Hello, son, I'm Felix, the janitor around here. C'mon, let me get you out of here. You've been holed up long enough."

I followed Felix slowly up the stairs to the main floor. As my eyes adjusted to the light, I was able to get a better look at Felix the janitor.

Felix was a Black man with a weathered deep brown face and short, wiry black hair that was gray at his temples. He was wearing a Western snap shirt and a pair of baggy, thick denim coveralls.

Felix said, "There is a slice of bread under your pillow. You better go fetch it before the mice get it."

He turned and limped toward the kitchen, then stopped and turned around to face me, as if he'd forgotten something. "Oh yeah, Sister Carolyn is looking for you. She is in the laundry room." Still looking me in the eye, Felix lowered his voice. "Play the game, son. Try to stay away from the infamous repentance cellar. It's not a good place to be. Especially watch your back around Joe Harvey. He's a snake in the grass, that one."

I nodded, letting Felix know I understood and I appreciated the tip.

I found Orson, Junior, and two other big boys sitting on chairs along the laundry room wall. From the looks Orson and Junior gave me, I knew I was showing quite a few bruises on my face. But it was the ones they couldn't see that hurt the most.

Sister Carolyn was a thin, gloomy-looking nun who never smiled. She said, "Alfred, it is your turn. Please take a seat."

Oh no! I hesitated to sit down, but I did. I thought, *I must play the game until the right moment.*

Sister Carolyn put a worn sheet over my shoulders. I had watched others get their hair cut, so I knew what was coming, but the first cut was the hardest. My scalp felt more naked with each strand of my long hair that fell to the floor.

"Ouch!" I flinched from the stink of kerosene that Sister Carolyn poured over my head. She said, "Just in case you have lice and nits or eggs."

Without my hair, I felt like I'd lost all my spiritual powers, and I wondered if I would ever get them back.

I heard Sister Carolyn say, "Orson High Elk, you're next."

I couldn't bear to watch. I knew how much it had meant for Orson to grow his braids back after the death of his grandfather three years ago. Plus, cutting our hair was reserved only for times we mourned our dead. And, to top it off, today was Orson's birthday. I thought, *How low can they go? Treating us like animals and cutting off our hair to kill our identity so they can give us a new one.*

I was certain I could hear the faint wailing of ancestors long gone as a heap of black hair piled up on the floor. Orson, Junior, and I spent the remainder of the day in mourning.

Days turned into weeks, and weeks into months. We spent the entire fall and winter with no visitors. One day in spring, I thought I saw my grandparents walking toward the main building, but by the time I found an excuse to go investigate, they were gone. I asked the nuns about it, but nobody seemed to know a thing. *Very strange,* I thought.

I was yearning for freedom, and I felt like a fuse on the end of a stick of dynamite. Orson said I was getting cynical, whatever that meant.

The dorm rooms were always cold, and many of the boys coughed all night. Many more cried themselves to sleep night after night. But not me. My tears were as dry as Coyote Creek in last summer's drought. I was ready to make that freedom run the moment fate opened her arms.

I tried to drift off to sleep, but the hoot owl calling outside my window made it impossible. Soon sleep came, and so did my visitor.

"Run, Big Heart! Run!" The voice was as crystal clear as the bell in the chapel tower.

Eyes wide open, I propped myself upright. "Who's there? What do you want?"

"Big Heart, you must run to the riverrrr . . ." The voice came from the foot of my bed.

Am I really hearing this? I asked myself.

After a quick scan of the row of iron single beds along the dorm room wall, the sound of deep breathing told me I was the only one awake. My racing heart let me know the ghostly voice was for my ears only.

"Wh . . . who are you?" I whispered. The only reply was the hoot of an owl somewhere on the other side of the bars on the window.

I sensed I was floating near the ceiling even as I cringed fearfully in the bed below. I could feel the familiarity, but I couldn't understand it, like the time I dreamed the roan stallion and I traveled through dimensions far beyond this world.

Stark blue-white moonlight spilled across my bed, illuminating an unusual shadow in the fold of the bedsheet. A large brown hand slowly took shape.

My eyes traveled up the arm to the face, and I gasped. My breath froze in the frigid air, like a whimsical white angel bringing tidings from the spirit world.

Oh no! It was my grandfather, and I could see right through him!

Scooting up straight, I whispered, "Grandfather, is that you?"

No answer, only silence and a blank stare from the two intense blue lights deep in his dark eye sockets.

His head slowly faded away into the moonbeam, followed by his body and lastly his hand, and my grandfather was gone.

I fell back asleep wondering why my grandfather would come to me in the middle of the night. Was it a warning? Did he see danger ahead for me?

Dawn broke, gray and bleak, with the sound of the dreaded wake-up bell. *Tink, tink, tink.* The horrible sound vibrated off the bare walls, right up to my bed, and right inside my head. I wished I could sleep another hour, but that was not an option.

"Ouch!" Limping with a stubbed toe, I slowly made my way to the outhouse. I sure wished the water was turned on so we could have indoor bathrooms again.

I did not have much time to wash up and get dressed before prayers in the chapel, so I rushed through my morning routine and hoped I wasn't too late. I ran through the dormitory doors to the front yard, using my hands to smooth down my coarse black hair. I was sure it looked like porcupine quills lying flat.

"Hi, guys. Glad you saved me a spot. I don't want to be late for our yummy breakfast," I said as I cut in line between Orson and Junior.

"Who doesn't love cold oatmeal sprinkled with specks of cooked weevils?" Junior snapped back.

Eyes Looking Back

The *tee-tee-tee* of meadowlarks in the hills above the school reminded me of home. Spring was here, and the days were getting warmer and longer.

At first I'd been excited, thinking maybe now my parents would come to take me, Elmer, Orson, and Junior back to Iron Nation. But I'd grown weary of watching the main gate at every opportunity, looking for my parents' black Ford Model A. I'd finally given in to the realization that they didn't care, and I was on my own.

Sister Rachel pushed and jerked us into two lines to march military-style to the chapel for morning Mass. Mass was always before breakfast, and it was the only time all of us students were together in one place. It was also a time to exchange news.

It was not good to get caught talking. But I'd figured out how to dodge the rule. I taught myself how to talk without moving my lips. Orson said I would make a good ventriloquist. Of course, I agreed.

I took a deep breath through my nose, raised my tongue near the roof of my mouth, and exhaled without moving my lips. I threw my voice to my right. "Hey, guys, look up there to the right. It's Joe Harvey."

Orson and Junior fought back a smile. They both looked toward the main two-story window where Joe Harvey stood. They confirmed they saw him with two blinks of their eyes, a secret code we'd devised to communicate undetected.

Joe Harvey was a thick-faced man with shifty eyes and fiery red hair. He was feared by all, including Father Roberts. Joe Harvey used any excuse he could muster up to work the kinks out of his leather whip. For some reason, Joe Harvey had picked me out and was determined to break my spirit, and I was determined not to let him.

Junior had a mischievous look on his face that meant there was no telling what he was going to do. He turned his face toward the window and pretended he was yawning. When the nuns weren't looking, he stuck his tongue out at Joe Harvey. Orson and I could barely stop ourselves from laughing out loud. It was hard, but we marched on in silence all the way to the chapel.

I was looking for my little brother, Elmer, amid the row of brown faces being seated in the pews, but I didn't see him anywhere. *Shucks,* I thought, *I sure hope he isn't sick again.*

The hushed solitude of my surroundings gave me a chance to think about my unexpected visitor. *Why did Grandfather come to me last night? Is everything okay? Where is Elmer in all of this? Why isn't he here? Did someone hurt him?*

A tap on my shoulder startled me. "Whoa!"

It was Sister Rachel. Her pinched pale face, tightly pulled back by her black-and-white habit, was so close I could smell the eggs and bacon on her breath.

She said, "Alfred, Father Roberts would like to have a word with you."

My eyes rolled upward at her. "Meeee?"

Sister Rachel's thin fingers cut into my shoulder. "Yes, you! Shhhh, quiet now. The children are praying. Now, get up and follow me."

Oh no, I thought. *If Joe Harvey saw Junior stick out his tongue, then I'm in big trouble.* Unable to hide my dread, I marched stiffly two paces behind Sister Rachel toward the school office.

"Please come in and close the door behind you," said Father Roberts. "Have a seat."

He motioned me to one of the overstuffed blue chairs in front of his desk.

I was sure my face showed my surprise at Elmer already seated in the other blue chair. I could tell by Elmer's clenched hands he was just as nervous as I was. Without a word, I took a seat next to Elmer and waited for the verdict.

Father Roberts held a paper that appeared to be a telegram in his hands. I knew immediately that the news in the telegram was about my grandfather, and I also knew exactly what Father Roberts was going to tell us.

Father Roberts cleared his throat and looked at us over his fancy-rimmed spectacles. "I regret to inform you both that your grandfather Thomas Plenty Buffalo passed away during the night."

He stopped and waited for the news to sink in. Both Elmer and I sat unruffled and unmoved by the news of our grandfather's passing. Father Roberts seemed a little disappointed by our lack of emotion.

He continued, "Your grandmother Lucille Plenty Buffalo has requested that you both return home for the funeral. She also requests that Orson High Elk and Junior White Hail attend as well. Apparently, she needs all the help she can get to give your grandfather a proper Christian burial."

Father Roberts cleaned his glasses and let out a tired sigh. "Felix will drive you to the reservation line, where a family member will pick you up. Now, go gather your belongings and meet Felix in the parking area in one hour. You are both dismissed!"

We loaded up in the school's 1925 Ford Model TT stake truck. Elmer rode in front with Felix, and Orson, Junior, and I rode in the back bed of the truck. We were on our way, back to the Iron Nation community to give my grandfather an honorable traditional burial, like one he would have wanted. I thought, *At this point, that is all that really matters.*

It had to be the brightest, saddest May Day ever. My gaze drank in the familiar landscape. The silhouette of Medicine Butte against the blue sky spread across yellow-crested rolling hills, then dropped down to the chalkstone bluffs that overlooked the beautiful Missouri River, the life source for my people.

The rhythmic rise and fall of the road soothed my mind. I went back in time and thought about last summer. It was the last time I'd spent time with my grandfather, and it was also when I'd finally fulfilled my vision quest, which I had avoided for many years.

It was mid-August, right after the White River Frontier Days and two weeks before school started. The spirits came in the night and danced around my bed. I knew it was time to go to the hill to vision quest. The next day I asked Grandfather about the visit from the spirits. Grandfather accompanied me to Pete Flying

Crow's home. I filled my sacred prayer pipe with willow bark tobacco, and I presented my pipe to Pete and asked him to help me. He accepted my request.

Late into the night, my mother helped me make many prayer ties for my quest.

At sundown the next day, I was left alone on the hill to cry for a vision.

The vision came the first night. Five spirits in the form of five giant beavers came to me. They showed me huge earthen dams that they would build along the corridor of our sacred Missouri River. Rising water swallowed everything in its path: medicine plants, animals, birds, and even the entire community of Iron Nation. The spirit beavers merged into the darkness in a burst of lavender and blue. The dawn came, and so did my grandfather and Pete Flying Crow. On the way home, Grandfather told me he was pleased that I'd finally fulfilled my obligation. Now, he could travel home in peace.

I hadn't known back then what he meant, but now I did.

This was a memory that I would cherish forever.

"Hoka!" Orson snapped me out of my thoughts. The truck tires hit the drought-baked dirt clumps going down the hill into the Iron Nation community. The road was empty except for us.

After a few hard bumps, I said, "We made it! We are home, boys."

Good to Be Home

W e drove straight to Grandmother Lucille's log cabin. Cars, buggies, horses, and dogs filled the front yard. I looked for my parents' black Ford Model A, but it was nowhere in sight.

Grandmother Lucille; her sister, my great-aunt Pearl Hand; and Junior's grandmother Irma White Hail greeted us at the front gate. It felt good to walk under the giant cottonwood tree I loved to sketch. A wave of warm tears and comfort hugs from countless people reminded me just how much Grandfather was loved and respected by so many.

Most of the folks left, except for Grandmother; Irma White Hail; and Irma's sister, Grandmother Ruth Flying Crow, Pete Flying Crow's wife. The late-afternoon skies turned dark and dreary. Grandmother Lucille lit her kerosene lamps, and the small kitchen lit up like a bright summer day.

I couldn't resist any longer. "Grandmother Lucille, where are my parents? Have they been notified? Why are they not here by now?"

I sensed something was wrong when she took longer than usual to reply. She fiddled with her round spectacles, then said, "You really need to talk to your uncle Jay. He will tell you what he knows. I don't know anything."

I didn't like her answer, but I guessed there wasn't much more I could ask at this point.

Grandmother Lucille motioned to us to come closer. "Let me look at you boys. I am shocked. You are all so thin. And Grandson Elmer, your chest is rattling like a gourd filled with little stones. Look at those bruises on your neck, and your hair is shaved off. Tell me, what has happened to you children?"

We told Grandmother Lucille every detail, and she was furious.

Grandmother Lucille said, "I am not letting you children go back to that terrible place. Albert White Bear is going to Lower Brule to pick up our rations. I will send a note by him to Superintendent Wright about this matter. I don't think Superintendent Wright realizes the horrific conditions taking place at that Indian school. If I must, I will write a letter to the vice president of the United States, Charles Curtis. He is from the Kaw tribe in Oklahoma. Surely, he will help us."

After the initial grief, anger, and tears, the energy lifted a bit. Grandmother Lucille retrieved four letters from her apron pocket and handed them to me.

She said, "Grandson, these letters are from your mother. I intended to give them to you in person. When your grandfather and I tried to visit you several times, Father Roberts would not let us in the main building, so we left. I went straight to Superintendent Wright and told him about it. He said he would pay the school a visit, but from what I heard, he never did."

Soon we were telling stories and laughing like old times—chasing away grief and uncertainty, if just for the moment.

Chepa was ecstatic and about did a backward flip when he saw me. He sniffed my pockets, then put his front paws on my legs, finally reaching up to lick my chin.

My heart filled with joy with no room for anything else. "Chepa dog! Howdy, Chepa boy."

Chepa practically knocked me over. His soulful brown eyes looked at me as if I were the only person that existed in his entire world. "Woof . . . woof! *Yelp!*"

Whoops, I'd hugged Chepa a bit too hard. I had to dig in the cupboard for a dog biscuit on that note.

The rattle of pots and pans filled the kitchen. Soon we were served our traditional chokecherry pudding, chicken soup, and wild peppermint tea.

The only sound was the crackle from the old woodstove, along with four hungry boys and a dog slurping their bowls like it was their last meal on earth. The smell of sage, cedar, and sweetgrass swirled in the air as Grandmother Lucille fanned us with her eagle feather. It was sure good to be loved again.

Chepa and I played with his sock toy until Uncle Jay showed up. With a gust of wind, the front door blew open, and Uncle Jay filled the doorway. Brown dust whipped around him and sprinkled his black hair.

"Whew! What a dust storm. It's 'bout as bad as I've ever seen. But I suppose it'll clear in an hour or so." Uncle Jay cleaned his feet on a woven gunnysack mat on the floor by the front door. He smelled like cedar and pinewood. "Look at you boys! Getting taller by the day. Give your old uncle a big bear hug."

We hugged him good.

"I am sure sorry about your grandfather," he said. "I will miss him greatly."

Uncle Jay was never shy about his feelings. I always wished I could be more like him than my father. Uncle Jay was my father's younger brother.

He was tall and lean and a good worker. Plus, he was a horse whisperer.

He told me I took after him, because I was a horse whisperer too. I always thought maybe I was the son Uncle Jay wished he had. All I knew was that Uncle Jay made me feel special.

Uncle Jay had taken up boxing during the Great War. After the war ended, he moved to Pittsburgh, Pennsylvania, and became a steelworker and professional boxer. After losing his young wife in an accident, Uncle Jay, being young himself, returned to Iron Nation. He never remarried.

He'd taught my brother and me everything we needed to learn about boxing. He said it would help keep us out of trouble.

Uncle Jay gave my head an affectionate pat, kind of like the pat I gave Chepa. "It is still blowing hard. I need to get Orson and Junior home while I can still see the road. I will visit with you tomorrow before the wake service, and we will catch up then. Okay?"

"Sure, no problem, Uncle."

Orson and Junior walked out the door and into the howling wind gusts with Uncle Jay. It was a good thing they all lived a short distance away.

It was just me, Elmer, and our grandmothers. Time to get pampered and catch up on all the local news. Not knowing any details, I kept waiting for my parents to walk through the door at any minute.

When I entered my old room that night, the flame from the kerosene lamp danced across the small space. I whispered, "I can't believe it! Everything is still here: my baseball glove, the animal carvings in the windowsill, the pencil drawings welded to the walls with my homemade glue from flour and salt, and the blue hair ribbon from my friend Sage's hair."

I sniffed the ribbon. "Holy cow!" It still smelled like the lavender she wore. It was enough to make my hormones shoot right through the ceiling.

I sure did miss Sage. My mother had noticed how much I liked her right off. She'd said, "Son, don't let this distract you. You are way too young to know about love. I am sure it will pass."

I knew it wouldn't pass. I'd been in love with Sage from the first time I met her. She was my secret hope.

Wow! This is the bee's knees. I pulled out the old cookie tin from under my bed. The bent lid wasn't too hard to pry open. Inside was a pocket knife, a baseball pin, two lead drawing pencils, and a real gold arrowhead my grandfather gave me last May for my birthday.

It was time. I seated myself on the worn braided rug in the middle of the small lean-to room. I opened my mother's letters and read each one twice, but it was the last letter that I read a third time. My mother's words did not sound too confident about their situation. With a wide yawn, I decided that I would read it again tomorrow.

It was a darn good feeling to be in my old bed and far away from St. John's and Joe Harvey.

"Good night, Chepa," I said to the fur pile lying at the foot of the bed. He raised one bristly eyebrow and was down for the count.

Morning came on the rays of intense sunlight glaring through the window. The storm had passed, leaving the land covered in drifts of brown dirt.

Grandfather's Journey and Our Return

I rode with Uncle Jay to the community hall for Grandfather's wake service. Elmer would ride with my grandmothers. It was a short ride.

Arriving at the community hall, we parked in the dirt driveway at the end of a row of buggies, cars, trucks, and wagons.

I said, "I guess we are late."

Uncle smiled over at me with a twinkle in his eye. "No, we are not late. We are on Indian time. It's always the right time when we show up." His face turned serious. "Nephew, do you want to talk about it? I know you are just as bothered as I am that your parents are not here."

"Uncle Jay, do you know if something happened to them?" I asked, thinking about the last letter I received from my mother.

Uncle Jay said, "I don't know, Nephew. But I do know my brother. If he received the telegram that I sent to the Sioux City police regarding your grandfather Thomas's passing, he and Grace would be here right now. The telegram was delivered to the last address your parents left me."

For some reason I didn't tell Uncle Jay about the letter. He might have wanted to take it from me, and it was all I had of my mother to hold on to. Heck, it even smelled like the lavender oil she used.

Uncle Jay's eyes had a faraway stare. He tapped his fingers on the steering wheel knob. "It's probably nothing. Come on! Let's go in. We have a wake to help with."

The wake was a beautiful tribute to my grandfather's life. It gave family and friends a chance to process his departure. Everyone but me. He'd left me holding a basket full of the future we could have made together but now never would. Plus, he'd never tried to stop my parents from sending Elmer and me to St. John's Indian School. And now it was too late to hear his side of the story.

The morning of the funeral came much too soon. I struggled to keep in step with the other pallbearers.

"You fellows watch your step." It was Joe Driving Hawk, holding the door open for us. Joe used to be my grandfather's best friend.

The narrow doorway of the Messiah Episcopal Church was barely wide enough to carry the casket through. Struggling against gusts of wind, we carried the casket a short distance to the Iron Nation cemetery.

The crudely cut grave stood out as a gaping black rectangle in the Dakota ground. Lakota honor songs and Episcopal hymns synchronized with the high-pitched wailing from the women. The clouds opened wide, and a brilliant sunbeam shimmered through the wings of a golden eagle circling above our humble gathering. It was the sign I'd been looking for. I knew the ancestors had come for my grandfather; he was now on his journey with them to the spirit world.

Grandmother Lucille pulled me aside during the funeral feast. "Grandson, Superintendent Wright has allowed Elmer to stay home with me. But you, Orson, and Junior will have to return to St. John's Indian School to finish the school year out. I wish I had better news." She wiped her eyes and squared her shoulders strongly. "Superintendent Wright said he would personally check on you boys. I must believe that."

I knew Superintendent Wright was a liar. We were just another number on an Indian census, and he would never make a visit to the school.

The day after the funeral, it was time to return to St. John's. I made sure I put my mother's letters safely inside the cookie tin under my bed. All but one. I pushed the last letter deep inside my trouser pocket and joined Orson and Junior in Grandmother Lucille's kitchen. Wisps of blue smoke from smoldering sage, cedar, and sweetgrass filled the room. Grandmother Lucille lined us up and smudged us all in turn, from front to back and up and down.

She said, "Good. I want you boys to always remember that you are Lakota warriors. The spirits will make a way for you."

Grandmother Lucille's face was drawn and sad. I knew she would mourn deeply for the next year for my grandfather, the man she'd married when she was a teenager.

She sighed. "Don't you boys worry. I am working on getting the day school opened again. Grandson, you especially don't worry about Chepa and Anpo, or us for that matter. We will fare just fine. We still have your grandfather's red tractor, and your uncle Jay is a big help."

I nodded while trying to swallow the big knot stuck in my throat.

Ahooga! Ahooga! Uncle Jay pulled up in the front yard in his Chevy truck. He leaned out of the driver's-side window and shouted over the idling engine, "You boys ready?"

I answered. "Not really, but here we are."

Uncle Jay had attended a residential mission school in his youth. I was certain his memories weren't a bed of roses either. But, just like us, Uncle Jay had no good way to beat the system and went along with it.

Off we went toward Kennebec, a small town located twenty miles south of Iron Nation. Felix was parked in front of a dust-choked filling station. We had no formal goodbye in our community, so I just said "See you later" to Uncle Jay, and we climbed in with Felix.

"Where's my buddy Elmer?" Felix asked.

"He's sick, and Superintendent Wright allowed him to stay home for the rest of the school year," I replied.

"I reckon that is the best place for him," Felix said.

By the looks on our faces, I was sure Felix knew we dreaded going back to St. John's Indian School. But the law was the law.

The first thing I did when I was back at school was hide my medicine bundle and my mother's letter in my secret place: beneath a loose wooden plank under the leg of my cast-iron bed. I believed it was safe there.

Conditions at St. John's Indian School were worse when we returned than when we had left. Along with disconnected electricity and limited access to water, food was scarce as ever. While we were gone, two little girls had died from scarlet fever. Now, added to everything else, we had another outbreak of the fever.

We jumped right back into our work. Not much schooling was going on beyond repairing buildings, digging up waterlines, and chopping wood and hauling water.

Exactly two weeks after my grandfather's funeral, my birthday arrived: Sunday, May 24, 1932. I decided that after Mass I would bring my medicine bundle to the river for a water ceremony that included a prayer and a blessing.

The sun was overhead when Orson and Junior joined me at the river. I pulled my medicine bundle out from my trouser pocket. Holding it in my hand, I offered a prayer to the water people and asked for blessings.

I finished up quickly to avoid being missed and someone seeing us. *Too late*. Joe Harvey was running down the embankment toward us.

He shouted, "What're you boys doing? You look like you are up to no good again!"

"Jump him!" I shouted.

Orson, Junior, and Joe Harvey tangled together in a heap and went rolling down the embankment like one big oak barrel. Wasting no time, I ran directly to my dorm room and hid the bundle back under the floorboard. I slipped out the east door toward the woodpile. I started chopping wood, which was one of my chores for the week.

Joe Harvey tackled me from behind, and I went down. Father Roberts, watching us from his office window on the second story, raced down and stopped our fight.

Joe Harvey told Father Roberts that Orson, Junior, and I were praying in Lakota at the river. Since practicing ceremonies and speaking Lakota were strictly prohibited, all three of us were locked up overnight in the infamous repentance cellar. We took the opportunity to catch up on the rumors being passed around the big boys' dormitory.

Orson said, "I heard that the bank in town collapsed, and St. John's Indian School lost all of its financial income."

I said, "Of course. That explains why there is not enough food to eat and no money to pay for electricity."

"Which caused the water pipes to burst this past winter," Junior piped in, "and here we are, still hauling water from the river."

I lowered my voice just in case the walls had ears. "Last week Father Roberts and two of the nuns carried the bodies of two little girls from the sick room. Felix said they passed away from tuberculosis and scarlet fever. Perhaps even malnutrition." Looking around, I continued, "Felix also said that Father Roberts is considering keeping all of us students here through the summer into the next school year so the school can recoup its losses."

Orson let out a heavy sigh. "I sure don't like that news one bit. It seems to be getting more dangerous day by day."

Things Are About to Change

isten up!" I whispered. "One good thing this old school has taught us is how to use tools and work like grown men."

Orson and Junior nodded their heads in agreement.

I continued, "I'm fifteen years old, and I am ready to break free from this place. Plus, we have skills we can use. If we stay, we surely will die from hunger, scarlet fever, or being beat up by Joe Harvey."

I could hear Orson running his fingers through his coarse, short haircut. "I hear you, but where are we safe? Where can we go that the government officials can't find us and bring us back here? The schools get a lot of money from the government to make us into mainstream Americans. They will look for us with a fine-tooth comb. I am certain of that."

Junior piped up. "You both know that the first place they will look is in Iron Nation, so we can't go there."

I told them about the message my grandfather had brought to me from the grave, telling me to run to the river. That the river would guide me to safety.

Junior said, "Heck yeah! We can trick the Indian police, Father Roberts, Joe Harvey, and the deputies from town who will look for us. I can see it now! We will trick them all! Buuuut . . . when do we do this, Alfred?"

Both Junior and Orson waited for a definite answer.

All I could say was "I don't know exactly, but when the time comes, the Great Spirit will give me a sign, and I will know what to do."

Junior said, "Alfred, do you ever doubt yourself? Like, maybe it is not really a sign from the Great Spirit but your own imagination?"

Scratching my head, I said, "I must believe in something and stand by it. Right? So I choose to believe that the Great Spirit sends his helper spirits to guide us if we pay attention to the signs around us."

Junior nodded.

I said, "Back to our plans. Perhaps we can borrow a boat from the ones tied up under the bridge in town. I think our best bet on escaping is drifting downriver."

Orson said, "I think we should hitchhike and go east as far as we can. We might even make it to Minnesota."

I thought, *But I want to follow the river to Sioux City and find my parents. Besides, I am sure that is what my grandfather's spirit was telling me.*

Junior perked up. "I'll go along with either plan. I'm sure we can find work wherever we go and disappear into the crowd. Shucks, I think the authorities will eventually grow tired of looking for us."

I softened my voice. "Most important thing here, guys, is that we stay together on this and make sure we have enough food to stay hidden and survive."

Orson let out a long yawn. "I have two cans of beans and a piece of flint to make a fire buried in the tree grove near our worksite. Might help some."

"Me too," Junior said. "I have three cans of milk hidden in the crevice of the rotten tree trunk in the same grove."

"Well," I said, "I don't want to outdo you, but I have a small sack of dried deer meat and some dried plums hidden that Felix passed to me. I think he knows we are planning to escape. I think he wants us to escape."

We all agreed that any direction we traveled sure beat staying here.

Felix showed up early the next day and let us out of the repentance cellar. Father Roberts was determined to get the windmill fixed by the end of the week. Since he was short on help to finish digging the trench, he'd let us out of the cellar.

Maybe it was fate, or my grandfather's hand from the grave. Either way, things were about to change. Dawn painted a path for us in the eastern sky with a mix of pinks and lavenders. Orson, Junior, and I joined Luke and Merle to finish digging the trench from the windmill to the main building.

I was carrying more than my share of tools, a pick on one shoulder and a newly sharpened shovel on the other. I looked up at the squeaky windmill, and I missed my step. I fell into the half-dug trench, right on top of the tools I was carrying.

"Whoaaaa!" I felt the leg of my worn denim overalls tear as I tumble down on top of the shiny shovel. The pain jabbed into my left shin.

Junior's eyes looking down at me popped wide. "Are you all right? Looks like you might have quite a gash there."

Orson reached down and helped pull me out of the trench.

"Yup! Looks bad," Orson said. He pulled off his bandanna and wrapped it around my leg, then pointed toward the main building. "You need to get to the school nurse and get that leg stitched up." Leaning in, he whispered, "Especially for what is up ahead."

I nodded. "I agree. I will go find Sister Regina. Just hope Dr. Garrison is not there!"

Dr. Garrison was an army doctor who usually made his rounds on the last Monday of the month. It seemed Dr. Garrison had operated on practically every single student, with the exception of a few of us—like Orson, Junior, and me—who stayed clear of him at all costs. He was noted for taking out tonsils and operating on perfectly healthy eyes, especially on days he overindulged in Father Roberts's sacramental wine.

My entire leg was throbbing at this point.

It didn't help matters that I ran into Joe Harvey on my way up the steps.

He pushed me down the last two steps and kicked me hard. I jumped up . . . Maybe it was perilous, but I was tired of being bullied. No more! Anger growled and scratched at my belly.

I faced Joe Harvey with my hands up in a boxing stance.

"Come on, you big bully! I'm not afraid of you!" I shouted up at him, his red face gloating in anticipation of the pleasure of seeing me squirm.

I could hear Uncle Jay deep in my head: *Keep your guard up, don't assume your opponent's next move, duck with the punches, and stay light on your feet, boy.*

In less than a minute, I was sprawled on my back, wearing the imprint of Joe Harvey's thick fist on my cheek.

Holding his foot on my leg, Joe Harvey sneered down at me. "Hope you know I'm through being nice to you, kid. No one opposes me and gets away with it. One more student buried out back just might not be a bad idea after all . . . Ha ha."

Blood was about as thick on my lips as it was soaking up my pant leg. I waited until the *click-clap* of his shoes faded into the stone floor before I stood up. I hobbled toward the main building to find Sister Regina.

Father Roberts met me in the hall. "Is everything okay? You look like you've just seen a ghost."

I nodded yes and mumbled, "I need Sister Regina to look at my leg. I fell into the trench by the windmill and cut it. It hurts badly."

Father Roberts looked closely at my bloody trouser leg. "You're right, it looks like it needs some attention," he said. "Come this way. I will take you to her and Dr. Garrison."

Oh no . . . not Dr. Garrison. I am having the worst luck ever. I struggled to keep from running in the opposite direction like a rabbit running for cover.

"My goodness, Alfred, you are truly a blessed boy," exclaimed Father Roberts. "You must know Dr. Garrison is only here on special days, and today is special. I am sure he will fix up your leg like new."

On the Run

Sister Regina was alone in the clinic. *Thank goodness.* Maybe my luck had just changed for the better.

She said, "My goodness, that is quite a cut. But I have seen worse. I don't know where Dr. Garrison is now, but I'm going to put a couple of sutures in that leg. I'm sure that is exactly what he would do anyway."

She applied a square cotton cloth seeped in an anesthetic solution to my open wound.

"Oooouch!" My voice cracked. "That stings like the dickens."

Sister Regina went to work with sutures attached to the eye of a needle and pulled double strands through my skin on both sides of the wound. After several passes, the gash was securely closed. She put a thin layer of ointment over the area. Finally, she gave me a hefty shot of penicillin, just to be on the safe side.

The double doors to the sick room swung open, and Dr. Garrison made his entrance. I could smell alcohol on his breath. He was a little tipsy.

"What do we have here . . . hmmm . . . What happened, young man?"

I mumbled something.

I was sure he wasn't even listening to me as he turned my leg over, from one side to the other.

He said, "This leg sure doesn't look good, even with those half-done sutures sewed in. It sure looks like a bad case of osteomyelitis, a bone infection. That leg needs to be removed. Yes, it needs to be removed! Sister Regina will prep you for emergency surgery."

"What? I just cut it! How could it be infected? I just cut it!" I panicked.

Dr. Garrison ignored me and left the room to get his infamous medical saw to cut my leg off.

Sister Regina stood motionless; her face was pale, like she was going to faint. She was just as horrified as I was. She stuttered, "Son, you need to get away from him. I'm sure he will sober up and not even remember you. Go now!"

This was it! It was time to run. Everything exploded into complete chaos. I needed to run like my life depended on it, because it sure did.

Still in my hospital gown, I grabbed my work clothes piled on a nearby table: a red-and-blue plaid cotton shirt, my blood-stained overalls, and my brown corduroy jacket. Sister Regina hastily handed me my leather work boots.

I skipped lacing my boots, instead stuffing the laces and my feet into the shoes, and ran for my life right through the double doors. Right smack into Dr. Garrison. The surprise collision sent him sliding across the freshly disinfected floor with his medical saw tightly clenched in his hand.

I kept on running.

"Get him. Grab him now!" Dr. Garrison screamed at Sister Regina. She didn't budge.

I heard a loud click behind me. I took one look to make sure it wasn't a shotgun aimed at my bare behind. It was Felix. He had locked the sick ward door from the outside—locking Dr. Garrison and Sister Regina inside.

I always knew Felix was on my side. He handed me a green canvas bag that had a wide shoulder strap sewn on the side.

"Been saving this for you. Knew you'd run sooner or later. There is some grub and other things inside the bag. Son, you need to get the heck out of Dodge while the gettin' is good." Felix tipped his hat in respect. "Good luck, son. I hope you make it!"

I gave him a thumbs-up and ran for my dorm room. Prying the wooden plank under my bed

loose, I retrieved my medicine bundle and letter.
I slipped the leather thong around my neck and
rammed the letter deep into my pocket. I ran
limping out the side door and made a beeline
toward the windmill to get Orson and Junior.
When I was within hearing range, I shouted,
"NOW! It's time to make the run! We must go
now!"

Orson, Junior, Luke, and Merle stared with
shocked, gaping faces.

It didn't take long for it all to soak in. Orson
and Junior grabbed their jackets and gloves. The
three of us ran farther down to the grove of trees
to retrieve the rest of our canned goods and my
dried meat and plums. We crammed the canned
and dried food and the flint into the green canvas
bag and headed out. We had to decide fast! We
ran east until I veered south toward the river with
Orson and Junior on my tail.

"HOKA HEY!" Our battle cry ricocheted all
the way from the chapel tower right down to the
bowels of the repentance cellar.

I knew we had a good head start, but soon
enough, Joe Harvey and his dogs and whoever else
was in on the chase would be on our trail.

I shouted, "Look over there! Looks like a small
boat tied to a tree. Quickly, let's get the boat and get
it into the river!"

Without a moment to spare, we were paddling out into the strong current of the Missouri River. The bow of the boat cut into the whitecaps along the surface of the dark water. The wind whipped against my face. I rowed with all my strength, in rhythm with the churning water splashing over the hull.

Miles downriver, the water unexpectedly exploded a few feet in front of us. A long narrow trail of ripples suddenly burst across our path. Breaking the surface of the water was a prehistoric-looking creature twisting and turning from side to side. *Whew!* It was only a sturgeon but the biggest one I had ever seen.

The boat turned from the uneven distribution of our weight and heaved toward a sandbar. The boat capsized, and we went overboard. I was the first to kick my way to the surface. In a few seconds, Junior and Orson surfaced next to me.

Gasping for air, I shouted, "Swim to the shore!" I gulped in a large amount of river water and went under again. The next time I surfaced, I latched on to a piece of driftwood nearby. Freeing myself from the grip of the rapid current, I was able to swim toward the riverbank.

I crawled out of the water and tried to stand. I couldn't do it. I fell back down and lay on my back in the sand until I caught my breath. I sat up, hoping I would see Orson and Junior next to me. But I didn't see either one of them.

My heart raced. "Please, Great Spirit, let them be okay," I prayed. "Orson? Junior? Where are you?" I called through my cupped hands.

"Over here!" Orson answered.

I staggered over to him. He was lying on his back on the sandy shore, wet as a mallard duck but very much alive.

Not too far from him was Junior, spread-eagled in the sand. "I'm here too. I'm okay. Just trying to dry out."

I felt tired but hopeful. Trying to encourage them, I said, "Let's not forget we are Lakota warriors! And we are still here!"

That was all it took! Orson and Junior perked up. "That's right!"

I said, "Looks like we lost the backpack, and I know we are hungry, cold, and tired. But it is critical that we keep moving. Most likely, we have a bounty on our heads."

I helped Orson up. He said, "You are right. We have to put some miles between us and Joe Harvey. And anyone else who is tracking us."

Hitchhiking

Hey, look over there!" Junior ran toward the green canvas bag, which had washed up on shore. He rummaged through it. "Wow, look at this! The tins kept the food pretty much dry. And the canned goods are still here too."

I said, "The canvas looks like it has extra wax worked in, making it extra waterproof. That Felix thought of everything."

Junior pulled out the dried pemmican, dried plums, and Johnson Café soda crackers. Another pouch held four cans of Cudahy's Vienna sausage, one can of beef and gravy, a canvas canteen, a knife, and a rope—plus a few other items Junior and Orson had put in the bag.

We were starving. It didn't take us long to gobble up two cans of the Vienna sausages with a few of the soda crackers and a few sips of water.

Still soggy from river water, I said, "For some reason, I'm not very thirsty." We had a good laugh at that one.

After appeasing our growling stomachs, I carefully pulled my mother's letter out of my pocket and opened it up. Good! The ink was blurred, but it was still readable.

"What is that? Is that a letter?" said Orson.

"Yes, it is from my mother," I answered.

"What does it say?" asked Junior.

I'd read the letter so many times I had it memorized. "I'll read it to you later. Let's just say it concerns me a lot."

A look came over Orson's face like he'd just hit on an idea. "Bet your mother and father are in trouble, and that is why they did not show up at the funeral!"

I wanted to punch him in the mouth for even saying that. But he was only saying out loud what I had been thinking all along. "Maybe you're right, Orson, but maybe not. I'm sure we will eventually find out."

Orson said, "I guess the idea of floating down to paradise isn't feasible. Looks like we need to change our plans. Time to get up on that highway and hitchhike."

"Let's go!" said Junior.

It was midafternoon, and the sun was hanging in the western sky. Our clothes were completely dry. Shucks, our leather boots had even stopped squeaking.

"My leg feels like a dozen buffalo just ran over it," I said. "I don't think I can walk much longer. I sure hope we get a ride right away."

We'd just reached Highway 16 when we spotted a car coming in our direction. Orson and Junior voted for me to be the one to flag the car down. I was outnumbered and put my thumb in the wind.

The 1929 Henry Ford Model A slid to a standstill. A muscular man with sandy hair, tattoos, and a thick British accent shouted over the engine noise, "Come on, boys, get in if you want a ride! Long drive ahead!"

Orson and Junior slid into the back seat, shoulder to shoulder, and I slid into the front seat.

The man behind the wheel bellowed, "Howdy, I am Sir Harry Smith, but everyone calls me Lucky. Whom do I have the pleasure to meet?"

I said, "I'm Alfred, and these are my friends Orson and Junior. We are traveling east to look for work."

Lucky's stained teeth were clamped down tightly on a thick cigar that refused to stay lit. "Pleased to meet you boys. How old are you all anyway? Where do you all plan to work?"

Caught off guard by all the questions, I choked on my words.

Junior jumped in, but he made our made-up story more unbelievable than ever. "Ummm, we are eighteen. Don't know just yet where we'll be working but figured we could find something."

Lucky eyed us. He knew we were on the run and scared silly. "I take it all three of you are eighteen, correct?"

Yup, that's true. We are all eighteen," I answered.

"Me, I work at finding people. Right now, I am working as a carnival caller for an amusement park in Sioux City, Iowa. Do you boys know what a caller is? Cripes, I bet you boys haven't even been to a carnival before, right?"

My heart was racing. *Is he an undercover agent sent to find us?*

I looked sideways at Lucky. I was sure he could read the mistrust in my eyes. I said, "You are correct, sir. We have not had the privilege of attending a carnival."

Lucky said, "You know, being a caller is an art. I can call in most any passerby. It doesn't take long before I have them paying their hard-earned money to experience an exotic world of human marvels and entertainment oddities. Yup! It's an art."

Lucky rambled on and on, and I sank deeper and deeper into my thoughts. It should not be so easy for life to turn upside down in such a short time, but it was. It shouldn't be so easy for someone like my grandfather to just fall and die. But he did! I was trying not to be angry at our predicament, but I was. And now we might be in the hands of our enemy. That thought made my throbbing leg hurt even more.

Bucking an eastern wind, we bumped down the highway toward the unknown. I settled back into the dusty seat cushion reeking of stale cigar smoke. I was excited and cautious at the same time because I had never been this far east before.

Orson talked a mile a minute when he was nervous. It was obvious he was very nervous and rattled on and on about everything under the sun, while Junior shot me side glances loaded with questions.

The road switched from dirt to gravel in a few areas. We stopped and started again and again. The hills disappeared into a flat sea of yellow and green prairie grass. I kept scanning the prairie landscape for the best place to make a run for it.

A familiar sensation slowly rose from the pit of my stomach. I pushed it away. *I won't miss any of them, not my grandfather in the spirit world, not*

Chepa, Elmer, my parents, Anpo, the roan, or Sage and my family at Iron Nation. I won't!

I must have been gritting my teeth, because Lucky looked over to see if I was okay. I looked back. A cigar-smoke halo swirled above Lucky's head. A thick crooked scar cut into his partially closed left eye. He had two more scars on his right arm from his wrist to his forearm. I wondered why they called him Lucky with so many obvious hard knocks.

As if reading my thoughts, he said, "Take it easy. I am not going to hurt you boys. You can trust me. Heck, I can even line you up with some carny work if you want. We are always in need of extra help. What do you think?"

I leaned back toward Orson and Junior. I didn't even need to ask them, because I could tell by the looks on their faces that they were in.

I said, "We've decided to take you up on your offer. We will work the carny circle until we get a little bit of money tucked away. Of course, this is all new to us."

Lucky grinned from ear to ear. "No problem, boys. You will get paid when each gig is over. The owner, Jack Johnson, sometimes gives advances. I would advise you not to do it, because Jack can be brutal, and he will end up owning your soul . . . just saying."

I thought, *Lucky sounds as though he has been down that road before.*

I clutched the door arm in horror as a car in the middle of the road came right at us. *Ahooga! Ahooga!* The car horn did no good.

Lucky shouted, "Watch out! The car's going to hit us! Brace yourselves, boys! We are going down!"

Sioux City or Bust

ucky gunned the motor and turned the steering wheel to the right and then back to the left. The oncoming car sped past us!

In a cloud of flying gravel, we lunged toward the ditch. We were airborne, along with a sea of flying gravel that blocked out the sunlight. The Model A balanced sideways on two wheels until we hit a low embankment and stopped short of a complete rollover. The car landed upright on four wheels, and the radiator hissed in time with a singing meadowlark.

We wasted no time climbing out of the Model A onto solid ground. Lucky was sweating profusely, and his face was beet red. He said, "Is everyone okay?"

We brushed the dirt off ourselves. I said, "Yup, we are okay. What about you? Are you okay?"

Lucky cussed a blue stream through the smashed cigar still in his mouth. "In all my born days I have never had a road toad run me over like that. I want you to know that driver was either blind as a bat or boiled as an owl on hooch. We are darn lucky, boys, but from the looks of my jalopy here, we've been drawn through a knothole."

I said, trying to calm him down, "Lucky for us you're a darn good driver. Now I know why they call you Lucky."

"That's the damn truth," said Lucky.

He rolled his sleeves up and handed Junior his canvas canteen. He motioned toward a small artesian pond down the hill a bit.

"You boys go over yonder to that water hole and get us some water for the old jalopy's radiator. Make sure to let the mud settle off the top now. Meanwhile, I'll get to work changing out this blown-out tire." Lucky kicked at his tire. "Darn good tire too. What a tootin' shame."

Junior, Orson, and I walked toward the pond. I thought, *I sure don't want Lucky to find out about my wounded leg. He might ditch us if he thinks I might be a burden to him.*

Out of sight of Lucky and his jalopy, I sat down on a rock in the shade of a tall tree. I said to Orson and Junior, "Hey, you guys go on without me. I'm going to rest my leg a bit."

"Sure, no problem."

They both went on without me. Only a few seconds had passed when I felt something burning into my back. I turned around, and there it was! I blinked and looked again. The apparition was still there.

A shadowy mist in the shape of a man. I immediately recognized the long silver braids, the broad brown face, and the curve of the cheekbones.

It was the ghost of my grandfather, to show me something or maybe warn me.

The apparition slowly faded. The wind sent leaves and plant matter swirling around me. A few seconds later, it was as still and calm as a midsummer's night.

I couldn't believe my eyes! At the base of the rocks were several medicinal plants. I recognized echinacea and plantain right off the bat.

I didn't waste any time. I offered a small portion of pemmican to Mother Earth and took to picking the medicines. I first gathered the echinacea, with the pale purple flowers and dark brown cones. The echinacea had long stems covered with bristly short hairs.

I quickly gathered the large oval green leaves from the nearby plantain plants, which were distinguished by their central flower spikes covered in tiny transparent flowers.

Working quickly, I chewed the plantain leaves into a mouthful of mush. I pulled my pant leg up. The gauze had long since fallen off, and my sutures were crusted and red. I spit the chewed-up mush into my hands and packed it over my sutures. I wrapped my leg with my bandanna. At first, the plant stung a bit, but then it felt soothing.

The echinacea flowers and stems tasted sweet. I chewed and swallowed a handful to boost my healing process. I was sure my plant relatives and the hefty shot of penicillin Sister Regina had given me would help me fight off any infection.

It was obvious why my grandfather had come to me; he'd wanted to show me the medicines. I stuffed handfuls of plantain leaves and echinacea flowers and leaves inside the pockets of my jacket and pants.

I made a prayer of gratitude to Mother Earth for sending her children to me, to my grandfather for guiding me to these medicines, and most important, to the Great Spirit for keeping us alive.

Orson and Junior showed up just as I finished my prayer.

"Ready to go?" Orson patted me on the back.

"Sure, ready as ever!" I answered. I was feeling confident my leg would get better soon.

It didn't take long for Lucky to fill the radiator with the pond water. He got his old jalopy back up on the road, and we continued eastward.

"Sioux City or bust!" he said, spitting a wad of chewing tobacco out the window and just missing Junior in the back seat.

I looked out the window for something interesting and eye-catching. Horses and wagons lined the ditches. Every now and then we either stopped or slowed down to let the workers shovel gravel onto the roadbed. I could only imagine what this highway would be like in the future.

I also could only imagine what it would be like to work at a carnival, because I had never been to one before in my life.

We passed a filling station. A sign said gasoline was eighteen cents a gallon. Without warning, Lucky did a U-turn.

"Hey, boys, I think my old jalopy needs a drink of gasoline. Plus, I could use a good snort too," Lucky said.

He made a fast exit to the right and pulled his jalopy in next to a tall, thin cylindrical gas pump. With a couple of jerks and sputters, we stopped. Gas was visible at the top of the pump under a white globe with the words *Mobilgas*.

The air through the open window was stifling. A lone dust devil danced in the long shadow of a swinging white enamel sign overhead. I was wishing that the red Pegasus horse could fly right off that sign and put me on its back. We would keep going until we were only a dot in the cloudless Dakota sky.

A redheaded boy my age with a freckled face crawled out from under a car secured on two wooden blocks. Wiping his hands on a rag the same color as his grease-soaked trousers, he asked, "Fill 'er up?"

Lucky spit a wad of chewing tobacco in an empty oil drum I was sure was a trash container. "Yes! Fill 'er up, lad. Give us the works."

Without a word, the redheaded boy washed the windows and checked the oil, radiator, and tires.

Lucky reached into the deep cubbyhole and pulled out a dollar bill. He winked and handed it to the gas station attendant. "Keep the change. Maybe buy yourself a soda pop on ole Lucky."

Lucky had us back on the road in no time at all.

"Here, you boys munch on these. I kid you not, you'll love them." Lucky handed me a Bing candy bar packaged in red paper and tossed the remaining two in the back seat for Orson and Junior. "These here candy bars are made right there in Sioux City. Best darn candy bars you ever had, if you ask me."

Lucky held the Bing in one hand, tearing it open with his tobacco-stained teeth, while the other hand skillfully maneuvered the round knob on the steering wheel. "Yup, we need to get going if we want to make Sioux City by nightfall."

We rode in silence for the next few miles, enjoying our luxurious treat. Chocolate was always good.

Carnival World

We peered out at the dimly lit houses dotting the brown landscape. More buildings appeared with each mile.

Lucky said, "Look at this city! It is teeming with opportunities, and we are going to grab them up, boys. He-he. Yup, prosperity ripe for the taking!"

I could see the railroad tracks, the extensive mills, the meat-processing plants, and everything else in between. The success of the city was maintained by the hub of railroads that crossed the city and went out to every sector of the nation. I could see why my parents had wanted to come to this place. The only problem was I needed to find them.

Turning onto River Drive, we left South Dakota behind when we crossed the Big Sioux River and headed toward north Sioux City and the railroad district, our destination. The headlights on Lucky's jalopy lit up the ditch line. A glow hung over the river mist, growing brighter the closer we got. We turned a corner in the road, and an eyeful of lights flooded my sight just as Lucky's jalopy stopped with a squeal of brakes.

"Well, boys, we made it. Welcome to River Run Park, a poor man's entertainment. And one of the best doll towns around," said Lucky.

Off a short distance, I could see tents and lights along a broad walkway that ran adjacent to the river. An array of music greeted us through the open windows. Squeals rose from the other side of the tents, where the amusement rides were located. I couldn't help but stare at the people walking, talking, laughing, and carrying stuffed animals and fluffy pink cotton candy. They all seemed so happy. It felt strange to me.

The most enticing blend of aromas greeted us. I could just about taste the roasting hot dogs, popcorn, candy apples, and burgers. It was sure different from the musty smell of old candles and mice that lived in the walls of St. John's Indian School.

Lucky didn't have to coax us to follow him. It was the enticing blend of unfamiliar noises ahead of him that we followed.

A single gas-lit lantern illuminated a blond-haired man with muttonchops, wearing brown riding pants and practicing with a whip. "Hey, my friend, good to see you back. Looks like you brought us some new blood. He-he, we'll see if they last longer than the other lads."

Lucky shook the man's hand. "Good to see you too, Charlie. Sure hope your family is doing well."

Charlie said, "They are great! In fact, we have a new act this year. I am sure the crowd will absolutely love it!"

The blond-headed man disappeared as quickly as he'd appeared. We passed four clowns juggling several brightly colored balls under the glare of a spotlight.

Orson winked at me. "Kind of looks like you, Alfred . . . big red noses and extra-long feet. He-he."

I thought, *Smart, but if we weren't in public, I'd pin you to the ground in seconds.* But instead, I just made the ugliest face I could muster at him.

"Look over there at the pretty lady with the wild blond hair. She is riding that shiny white stallion backward. *Wow!*" said Junior.

I said, "Shhhh. Remember we are new here. Just try not to become a spectacle."

Junior didn't hear a word I said. "Are those tightrope walkers? I heard about them from my grandmother."

We all stood starstruck, gazing at the two men and three women in sparkly blue-green tights, balancing with poles on a wire high above us. The glittered quintet hung from the heavens.

"Look at that!" I said, doing a one-eighty-degree turn.

To our left was a gigantic wheel that rose magically up in front of us. It was lit up like a big Christmas tree decorated with a hundred glowing candles.

The wheel turned slowly, around and around, rising up and down to a tin-can melody blasting from a black box at its base. The attendant was a gray-haired man with a black patch over his right eye. He seemed to control the wheel with a metal bar that was hooked to the black box.

The blaring music couldn't drown out the screams of delight coming from the sky. It was the most spectacular mechanical contraption I'd ever seen.

I said, "Given the smiles on people's faces, it appears the depression missed Carny Town in Sioux City, Iowa, a tad."

It was dark. We dropped our dazzle-exhausted bodies near Lucky's car. Just in time, Lucky showed up with an armful of blankets. A skyful of twinkling stars was the last thing I saw before I fell asleep.

"Rise and shine!" Lucky's boot nudged my leg. Pointing in opposite directions, Lucky said, "Outhouses are to your left and the food tent to your right."

The hot coffee and boiled eggs hit the spot. Lucky didn't waste time; he had us at Jack's tent before I knew it.

Jack threw the tent flap open. "Come on in, boys! I'm Jack, the one who manages this playground. Now, tell me who you are."

I went first. "I am Alfred Swallow, I am eighteen, and I am from Pierre, South Dakota."

"That was a mouthful. Glad to meet you, Alfred." Jack shook my hand.

Orson went next and then Junior. We all stayed to the same story. I was sorry I had to lie to Jack, but it was for our own good.

Jack said, "First rule! Everyone here has a job, and the job always gets done. Second rule! No matter what you see, hear, or know, you mind your own business, and they will mind theirs." He went down his list. "Each of you will get paid on commission at the end of the week, given the work you get done and how well you mind your own business."

Orson and Junior glanced at me sideways. I pretended I didn't see them.

Jack said, "Orson, I want you to work with the ride attendants on the midway. Also check the lights on each ride at the end of each day. And remember to keep a log. Junior, you can paint the fences in the midway, especially around the Tilt-A-Whirl. Also, all the frames around the sideshow billboards. The paint is behind my tent."

Junior said, "You bet!"

Jack turned to me. "Alfred, you look like a stout boy. I am going to have you take care of the horses. The stables are on the east side of the grounds." He flashed a posed smile. "I've got to get going, so welcome to the carny world, boys. You can sleep in the bunk tents near the horse stables, and if you have any questions, you can find me here most of the time."

Nudging Orson and Junior, I said, "Hoka! I guess we are now officially carnies."

They gave a good chuckle.

When I reached the stables, she ran right up to me. She was a beauty, a white Arabian horse.

A voice from inside the shadows of the stable door said, "Her name is Goldie. She is a well-trained pure-blood Arabian. She can dance every step imaginable: straight, side to side, and backward. She can even roll over with commands." The woman stepped into the daylight. She was a pretty Native American woman with a long black ponytail tucked under a worn straw hat, and she wore brown leather riding pants. "Hi. I'm Willow. What's your name? Where are you from?"

I said, "I am Alfred Swallow, and I am Lakota Sioux from Iron Nation, South Dakota. Are you Native American? How did you end up here?"

Willow said, "I am born from the Kickapoo tribe in Oklahoma. I ran away from Chilocco Indian School, also in Oklahoma, years ago. The only kind matron in the entire school helped me escape. I have never looked back, no reason to. I have been working around the area training horses. When people figure out that I am Native American, they look at me like I am invisible. Nobody bothers me, and I don't mind. It sure is better than getting beat on every day for no good reason except to beat the Indian out of me." She flashed me a dazzling smile. "So here I am."

I shook Willow's gloved hand. "Me and my friends are runaways too. I am hoping we can become invisible too."

Willow giggled and tipped her hat. "Nice meeting you, but I need to get back to work, and you probably do as well. I am sure we will meet again, Alfred Swallow."

It was lunchtime, and I couldn't wait to see Orson and Junior and tell them about Willow. Sweat trickled down my neck. Mother Nature was brutal today. The air was stifling, and heatwaves shimmered off the white tents mercilessly. Occasionally, a blast of cool air from the nearby Big Sioux River teased at me, offering a few seconds of relief.

"We're a hungry bunch today," Orson said, walking up to me.

Today we were eating flame-broiled hot dogs and cold bottles of cream soda from the midway food tents.

Between munches I said, "I met a Kickapoo woman named Willow at the stables this morning. She ran away from an Indian boarding school just like us. She has learned how to make herself invisible."

Orson wiped his mouth on the bottom of his baggy white T-shirt, one of the clothing items donated to us from the carnies. "Maybe this woman can teach us how to become invisible. We might have a better chance at surviving in a white world."

It was close to one o'clock, and the gates would be opening soon to let the crowd through. The energy was high, and every carny was as busy as a bee, all working for an invisible queen that demanded satisfying the pleasure seekers.

The gates opened every afternoon at one o'clock and closed at nine, unless one wanted to finish off their evening in the tents at the end of the boardwalk. That side stayed open most of the night. It was a hidden world that nobody talked about.

I said to Orson and Junior, "I'm going to ask Jack for a day off to go look for my parents."

Orson said, "I wouldn't do that just yet, my friend. It is too soon, and he is liable to throw us out."

I nodded. "Yeah, I think you are right. Plus, it gives us time to find out where the popcorn factory is located."

A white-faced clown with a sad smile danced by us with his overstuffed stomach almost bouncing out of control. The sight gave us a good laugh and snapped me out of my heavy thoughts.

I said, "These carnies are a mysterious bunch, but they sure can turn an everyday world into a wonderland of illusion and magic."

Junior said, "They just want to make people laugh. I guess that's their way of sharing their magic with others."

I said, "Yup, laughter is a *good* medicine. When I was growing up, my grandfather would tell me that humor is a powerful medicine and heals the heart."

Orson stood up. "Good words, Alfred. But we need to get going before the crowds get here."

The crimson sunrays were filling the western horizon when Orson and Junior showed up at the stables.

"Good timing," I said. "Let's go explore."

"Heck yeah!" said Junior.

Zigzagging through the carnival grounds, we were immersed in a world of colors, sounds, and smells, all blended in a dazzling collage: tents and props painted in bright colors, fast-spinning cars, carousel swings, colorful costumes, trapeze acts, trick horseback riders, trained bears, elephant acts, magicians, fortune tellers, white-faced clowns, sword swallowers, fire-eaters, lion tamers, and every human oddity imaginable.

We reached the midway, and the rides were in full motion . . . the Tilt-A-Whirl, roller coaster, parachute jump, Pretzel, and famous Ferris wheel.

Callers were calling people in, tempting them with games of chance and food concessions that lined the corridor of the grounds. The smell of popcorn, cotton candy, hot dogs, and candy apples made me hungry. But we couldn't resist checking out the commotion at the big wheel.

Tapping one of the tightrope walkers on the back, I asked, "What is the excitement about?"

Laughing at the look on our faces, she said, "That's Fanny and Fred, the dwarfs announcing their marriage to everyone carny-style. They are making the usual ceremonial loop around the big wheel."

Curiosity glued us to the spot. We watched the miniature couple dressed in their finest garb and ostrich feathers climb into the metal seat of the big wheel. The metal bar snapped over their laps, and a wedding march blared out of the black box. Up they went, higher and higher, into the night sky. All we could see was the bottom of their fancy-shoed feet. Their ride ended in a chorus of "Congratulations" from the bystanders.

"Come on, boys, you are up next!" Somehow, the gray-haired attendant had decided it was our turn.

Nudging Junior forward, I said, "This can't be bad. It's a free ride. Let's go!"

We put Junior in the middle, crammed ourselves into the metal seat, and pulled the safety bar over our laps.

Orson shouted to the attendant, "We are ready! Take us up!"

We slowly lifted upward into a purple heaven blanketed with endless stars. We were flying and whirling through the sky like three heroes who'd had their powers restored.

Choking on my words, I said, "Holy moly, this is about as exciting as buffalo bull snot." Orson and Junior let loose a laugh that rocked our seat.

The big wheel stopped when it reached the top. We sat quietly as the fierce winds rocked the seat like a teeter-totter.

I said, "Hey, Junior, are you scared or what?"

"Nope, not me." Junior's face and white knuckles clutching the bar told a different story.

Jabbing him good, I said, "Could have fooled me."

Orson said, "I think the operator might be messing with us. Maybe it's our initiation ceremony or something."

I said, "Let's make the most of a free ride and enjoy the view."

Orson said, "Wow, I didn't realize how big this city is and how many lights there are at night. Hey, Alfred, there's your friend Willow below, waving at us."

I looked down, and sure enough, it was Willow. I waved back.

Finally, the big wheel ride started turning, and we had our feet on the ground on the fourth loop.

The gray-headed attendant greeted us with a toothless grin. "Thought I'd initiate you boys since the carny family voted you in. Welcome, you're officially one of us now."

Orson whispered, "Should we laugh with happiness or cry with regret?"

We walked sideways, still dizzy, toward Willow. Laughing, I said, "Willow, I want you to meet my friends Orson and Junior."

Willow shook their hands. "Alfred mentioned you, and I wanted to meet you, so I tracked you down."

Junior said, "Nice to meet you. We are on our way to the boardwalk area. Would you care to join us?"

Willow threw her head back and laughed. "Goodness, no! I think you don't want to go there either—that's if you have any brains. I must get back to the stables. Nice meeting you two, and I will see you later, Alfred."

Tipping her hat, Willow left us in the dust, and we watched her walk away.

I felt embarrassed. I hoped my friends hadn't put their big feet in their big mouths.

Orson said, "Wow! She is pretty!"

Object of Wonder

We headed down a walkway. Light from the string of artificially lit bulbs revealed that the other side of the boardwalk was strewn with heaps of river debris.

Pointing at the litter, I said, "I guess the boardwalk helps to keep the river debris discrete from the carnival goers." At the far end of the boardwalk was a row of burlesque tents. Scantily clad women in feathers and glitter were lined up with locked arms and swinging legs, practicing a dance performance. This section of the carnival came to life after dark with high-stakes card games and gambling.

Orson said, "This is as far as I want to go. Lucky warned us to stay away from the burlesque quarters if we don't want to see and hear things that might be offensive."

I chuckled, "Okay, I don't want to witness any transgressions, so we better call it a night and head back to the stables."

Orson said, "It has been an odd day for sure. Can't imagine what tomorrow's going to bring."

Morning came much too early. I stayed in bed a few minutes to ponder the dream I'd had during the night. I held my medicine bundle in my hand and thought about the message I'd received from my spirit helper. His high-pitched voice vibrated through the thin veil that separated our worlds. *The holy ones will help to locate your parents . . . trust them . . . make a prayer offering to the river . . . they will come.*

The sun shone straight overhead, and the rays were intense. Orson, Junior, and I sat on a wooden bench in the shade, eating peanut butter sandwiches on fresh slabs of white bread.

I said, "I never knew peanut butter sandwiches could taste this good, or maybe it's just the flavor of freedom I taste."

Junior slapped his leg, and we hee-hawed at our own folly.

Lucky showed up. "How you boys doing?"

"Good," "Okay," "Great," we answered in sync.

"Good!" Lucky said. "Alfred, Jack has a painting job for you. You better go see him before he gives the job to someone else."

Within minutes, I was sitting across from Jack. He asked, "Are you artistic? Can you paint animals, people, and landscapes?"

I couldn't believe my ears. I said, "I am an artist, been one my whole life."

He said, "Great! I need someone to paint several murals inside the tunnel of love ride. The ride is part of my new gravity-propelled roller coaster that is being installed. The job pays well. I will just give you some extra cash at the end of the week. What do you think?"

"Yes! I will take the job painting your murals," I said.

"Done deal!" said Jack. "You can start tomorrow."

We were getting used to our new world minute by minute.

We stopped by the carousel and watched it slowly turn, immersed in an array of lights and music. I couldn't help but throw my head back and let out a good laugh.

Pointing toward the carousel, I said, "I'm tickled by the excitement on the faces of those country folks. You know, they rode for miles by horse and buggy to get to the carnival. Then they pay their hard-earned money to ride wooden horses round and round on a carousel when their real horses are tied up in the stables waiting for them."

Orson and Junior joined me in laughing at our silly observations.

Orson pointed with his lips toward the hills far away. He said, "Heck, they are probably just like us.

Letting the magic of this make-believe world soothe the harsh reality of the real one out there."

At that moment, a feeling I couldn't explain came over me. I felt pulled toward a red-and-white-striped tent with a bright green awning under a sign that read *Bob's Burgers—Best in the West.*

"Come on!" I said to Orson and Junior. "Follow me."

We walked up to the counter of the red-and-white tent.

"Ahem!" I cleared my throat to let whoever worked there know that they had a customer.

No response.

I said, "Heck, let's go."

A man wearing a red-and-white-striped apron and a lopsided white cap walked through the side door just as we were about to leave. He seemed embarrassed. "Sorry about that. The crowd was gone, so I went to my shed for popcorn." He dropped the brown gunnysack of popcorn kernels on the tent floor. "Want a bag of popcorn?"

I said, "Yes, sir, we do. How much?"

"That will be a nickel for three bags." The man with the lopsided cap overfilled three colorful red, yellow, and blue oil bags with big fluffy popcorn and handed them to us.

"Thanks." I handed him a nickel. His intense stare was making me uncomfortable.

He said, "What's your name, kid? Are you one of the new prats here?"

I said, "I'm Alfred, and these are my friends Orson and Junior. Yeah, we work for Jack. I'm painting murals and taking care of the horses. My friends help with the midway rides."

The man stepped around the counter. He wiped his long slender hand on his red-and-white-striped apron and held it out to us. "My name is Robert Cohen. Everybody calls me Bob. I have been flipping meat patties in this old tent since Jack started this gig five years ago."

I was the last to shake Bob's hand. His intense stare made me nervous. Something about it was disturbing to me.

"Where you boys from?" asked Bob.

I said, "Pierre, South Dakota." I felt it was important not to let anyone know that we were from the reservation.

Bob said, "Don't mind me staring, but you sure do remind me of a man that used to deliver popcorn to me. You look like a miniature replica of him. Plus, he was from South Dakota too. Just too strange for coincidence. Just can't get over it. Ha. I guess we all have a twin somewhere, at least that's what they say around these parts."

I just had to ask. "What did you say this man's name was?"

"I didn't," said Bob, "but I am sure his name was Elmer. Yes, it was Elmer Swallow."

The air was sucked right out of me, like someone had hit me in the pit of my stomach. I turned my head and faked a cough to hide my shocked expression.

"Yeah . . . I was getting to like him a lot, and he just stopped coming by. Shucks! I haven't seen him since," Bob said.

I could hardly contain my emotions. I tried hard not to stumble over my words. "Do you have any idea what happened to him?"

Bob craned his neck toward the front of the tent to check for customers. The coast was clear. Leaning his stocky torso against the tent pole, he lowered his voice. "Apparently, one of the card dealers used to work with Elmer at a popcorn factory."

I asked, "Is the popcorn factory very far from here?"

Shaking his head, Bob said, "It's about five miles east of here on Fourth and Pearl. The card dealer said it was the craziest thing. First Elmer's wife disappeared, and the next day Elmer disappeared. Nobody seems to know a thing."

I blurted out, "Bob, my name is Alfred Swallow."

"What? Are you telling me you are Elmer's boy?" Bob said.

I nodded. I was shaking like a leaf. Orson and Junior were staring at us in disbelief.

Rumor Has It

Bob whistled in disbelief. "Well, I'll be darned! Now that I think about it, Elmer did mention that he had two boys. Something about wanting to make some extra money to get his family back together."

By this time a line was forming under Bob's bright red-and-white sign.

Bob said, "Getting backed up out front. Going to get back to work. But I'm closing early tonight, so I can meet you boys down by the river around seven o'clock. I will try to find out more."

I was nervous, and my thoughts raced as fast as the churning waters in the Little Sioux River.

I said, "We better get back to our stations. I heard Jack can be hard-nosed when it comes to work."

Orson let out a loud whistle. "What a turn of events! If this man, Bob Cohen, is really telling the truth, then we might get some leads on your parents' whereabouts."

I said, "I think we need to believe Bob Cohen is the real deal and he is going to help us."

Junior was silent. I knew my parents' disappearance was triggering the trauma of losing his parents many years ago, and I knew he would work through it, like he always did.

The day passed quickly, and I was cleaning my paintbrushes when Orson and Junior showed up. We wasted no time and showed up at the river fifteen minutes early.

"Hey, boys, I figured you'd all get here early, so I took off early." Bob was walking down the bank toward us. "Brought some refreshments too. Cold Sioux City root beer sodas."

I didn't waste time guzzling the soda down and picking Bob's brain. "Please tell me what you know about my parents. What is the name of the man they worked for?"

Bob jumped right to it. "Rumor has it that Henry Emerson, owner of the Great Plains Popcorn Company, was in the service with Elmer. Something about Elmer saving old Henry's life during some battle in France. My informant said Henry asked Elmer to come to Sioux City and work with him for a year."

I said, "My father never talked about the war. I don't know much about his battles."

Bob looked around to make sure we were in the clear. "Henry is a widower with no children, and he planned on setting Elmer up in his company. Henry has a younger brother, Fritz, who is on the wrong side of the law."

"Do you think Fritz Emerson had a hand in my parents' disappearance?" I could feel my heart beating in my head.

Bob said, "Absolutely I do. Fritz hooked up with the renegade lawman Verne Miller. All the locals know that Fritz Emerson and Verne Miller are running an illegal bootlegging business right here in Sioux City. Lucky and the reformed Bureau of Investigation are currently watching Verne Miller like a hawk."

Orson said, "Miller, hmmm. That name sounds familiar."

"It should!" said Bob. "Miller was a lawman, a trigger-happy sheriff. After stealing a large amount of taxpayer money, Miller fled to the other side of the law. He's a force to be reckoned with because he knows the system from the inside out."

I said, "But where does Lucky fit in with all this?"

Bob said, "Lucky is a G-man, a government agent with the Bureau of Investigation out of the Twin Cities area. My informant said Lucky tracked Verne to his hometown of Kimball, South Dakota."

Junior said, "Outside of Kimball is where Lucky picked us up hitchhiking. Now it all makes sense."

Bob lowered his voice. "But I want to warn you boys! Lucky doesn't do anything just for the heck of it. He always has plans for everything. I guess from his eyes, that is the way a good government man should be. Regardless, you boys get your war paint on and stay alert!"

This was getting more confusing with each word. Lucky! A special agent! Why hadn't he sent us back to St. John's Indian School?

Bob continued, "My informant said Fritz and Verne were using the Great Plains Popcorn Company as a cover to transport barrels of alcohol disguised as barrels of popcorn."

"What does this have to do with my parents?" I asked.

"Now, I am just speculating, but I think your father accidently saw something he wasn't supposed to see. Fritz and Miller had to get rid of your father, and they used your mother as bait to lure him in." Bob stood up. "I think if the authorities had more proof that your parents were targeted by Fritz and Miller, they might be more willing to help investigate their disappearance."

"I have a letter," I blurted out. "It is from my mother right before she went missing. It might help."

Bob dropped his voice. "First and foremost, you do not let anyone know you have that letter until you can get it to the right person. Your letter might be able to help your parents in a very important way."

Orson jumped in. "When can we meet Henry? Where does he live?"

I knew Orson and Junior were just as concerned as I was about my parents.

Bob scratched his head. "Hmmm, what about early tomorrow morning before the crowds get here? You boys can ride with me. It's a short drive south of here."

I said, "Sure, we'll see you tomorrow."

Junior and I listened to Orson talk nonstop all the way back to Carny Town. I was already thinking about the next day when we ran into Lucky. Little did I know Lucky had other surprises as well.

"Just the boys I have been looking for," said Lucky. "Do I have a deal lined up. You'll never believe it. You remember that fight tent I told you boys about?"

Orson said, "Yeah, what about it?"

"Well, let me tell you. There's a big fight scheduled in two weeks, and all the tickets sold out. But the fighter from Chicago who was scheduled to fight the local champ, Max Stolz, just fell over dead. Lots of money on the table. I am good friends with the fight manager, and he is in quite a tizzy."

I said, "Okay, but what does this have to do with us?"

Lucky could hardly contain himself. "Alfred, remember you told me you were trained by the best, your uncle Jay? You are as solid as a rock, and I figured you could hold your own in the ring . . . and . . . well . . . Stolz is a super featherweight and close to you in weight. I sort of gave your name to my friend . . . and told him you were eighteen and trained by the best. Of course, I'm just taking your word. But get this! He put you in the main attraction. You're going to fight Max Stolz. What a stroke of luck! What do you think there, Alfred?"

I felt sick to my stomach. I thought, *I am a good boxer, but I am just a kid. I can't fight a grown man. Besides, Lucky's job is to make sure criminals get caught, not setting kids up to get hurt. And what if someone recognizes me, and they send me back to St. John's? Or I don't fight, and Lucky sends me back to St. John's? Who is going to help find my parents? This is not good!*

The Letter

Lucky said, "So, what do you think?"

I wondered how much money he had on this deal. Lucky hadn't given me very many options for compromising. With a small shaky voice, I said, "Okay, but I will have to use all my free time to train."

Lucky said, "That's the other part. You don't have to train. You are going to get paid to lose. In fact, the fight manager wants you to lose to give the locals some excitement. It will be good for his business to have a local winner."

My shoulders hurt like I was carrying the weight of the world. One side held my parents, and the other, Lucky's grand scheme.

The final coats of paint went on the tunnel of love mural. I said to myself, "Good! Now I can head to the stable and visit my favorite animal here, Miss Goldie."

Goldie nudged my arm, looking for her usual treats. My uncle Jay had taught me well about horses and how to talk with them telepathically. And they always listened.

Today I told Goldie about my parents. She nickered and threw her silver mane as if to say, *Jump on my back, and we will ride to the stars far away from here*. I said, "I wish we could fly away together, Miss Goldie, but I came to find my parents, and that's what I must do, but thank you for the offer, he-he."

Orson, Junior, and I rode with Bob in his truck toward the wealthy neighborhoods of Sioux City. The winds of change were biting at my soul.

I said, "Hey, Bob, do you know that Lucky has me scheduled to fight against Max Stolz?"

"Whistling gopher!" Bob almost hit the ditch. "Lucky has you fighting Stolz? I think he is using you as bait to bust Miller. Miller used to be a boxer, and rumor has it that Miller has never missed a ticket for a fight in this area. Miller has been hidden, but something like this could bring him out."

Bob looked across the front seat at me. "I also know that Lucky doesn't know a thing about boxing. You are going to need professional training. I might be able to help, but only if you want. I used to be a professional boxer in the service. Besides,

I'll savor the day that someone can put Max Stolz down. Perhaps that day is coming soon."

We passed through a large wrought-iron gate with *Emerson* etched in the arch above us. We drove past tall green pines that lined both sides of the drive. Pulling up in front of a two-story Victorian-style house, we parked next to a familiar truck.

Junior whispered, "That truck sure looks familiar."

Orson whispered back, "It should! It's Uncle Jay's truck."

Stunned, I said, "I wonder what he's doing here?"

Orson said, "Maybe the same thing we're doing, trying to find your parents."

We followed Bob right up the marble steps to the front door. He knocked on the fancy carved wooden door. *Knock! Knock!*

No answer.

Orson said, "Maybe we should use that shiny lever hooked on the door. I think it is a door knocker or something."

CLANG! CLANG! The door flew open, and I was looking up into the face of a big man with black glasses, dark brown hair, and a thick dark beard covering most of his face.

"May I help you?" the man said, looking us up and down. "For crying out loud, Bob, I didn't recognize you. What are you doing here? Who are these young men?"

I extended my right hand and said, "Hello, Mr. Emerson, I am Alfred Swallow, Elmer and Grace Swallow's son."

I feared Henry was going to fall over with the way he staggered backward. Bob was quick to grab the man's arm.

Henry's face was twisted with pain, probably more emotional than anything. "I'm okay. I was just a little shocked for a moment. Come on in. Let's talk."

We walked into a large well-lit room with big windows and an impressive carved ceiling.

Uncle Jay was standing by one of the big picture windows. He crossed the room in two strides. "Nephew Alfred, Orson, and Junior, I'm so sorry you boys had to run from that school. But I knew you would eventually make it out, and if you didn't, I was coming to help you escape. I have been here two weeks working with Henry. I think we have a few good leads. If only we had more evidence, we could get more help from the local authorities."

I replied, "Good to see you too, Uncle Jay! And we are pleased to meet you, Mr. Emerson."

Henry didn't beat around the bush one bit. "Son, please call me Henry. I am afraid your parents were abducted. And I fear it's not good."

Bob said, "Henry, Alfred has a letter from his mother, Grace. She wrote it right before she and Elmer disappeared. It might shed some light on things. It will explain everything that is happening right now."

I handed my mother's letter to Henry. "The ink is blurred, but I believe you can still read it." Looking at Uncle Jay, I said, "I'm sorry, Uncle Jay."

Uncle Jay looked confused as I handed my mother's letter over. Henry read the letter in silence twice over and finally out loud:

Dearest Son,

I hope you are good. I understand why you haven't answered my letters. You must be very busy learning and enjoying being with your friends. I mentioned in my last letter that I took a new job at the same popcorn factory that your father works at. The owner is good to us. Your father now drives a big truck and delivers popcorn and other items to businesses around town. I feel uneasy about telling you these things, but I need to let somebody know. I think your father and I are in big trouble.

Your father and I accidently overheard a man named Fritz Emerson telling another man, Verne Miller, that he'd had enough,

*and he was going to take the old man out
and your father with him. They both had
funny-looking rifles, and I think they plan on
killing someone. If we don't make it home by
summer, have Uncle come and look for us in
Sioux City. I sure didn't want to burden you
with my fears.*

*Good news! I have been saving our money
faithfully and have quite a bit saved up. I sure
can't wait for this all to pass and for us to be
together soon back home in Iron Nation.*

*PS: Please watch out for your little brother
and give him a big hug for me.*

Love you.

Your mother

You could hear a pin drop on the marble floor.

Bob broke the silence. "I think Fritz and Verne
might have Elmer and Grace holed up somewhere
in the vicinity. Most likely, they're planning on
demanding a ransom to force you to turn over your
estate to Fritz."

Henry let out a loud sigh. "You're absolutely
right, Bob!" Walking to the picture window, he
looked off into the distance. "I had a visitor yesterday
at noon. She showed up in a black Cadillac Town
Sedan and left me a note at the front door. Watching

her leave, I had a gut feeling I was about to get some disturbing news. And I did!"

Everyone in the room was hanging on Henry's every word. "And?"

He continued, "It was a ransom note. It said they want one hundred thousand dollars paid in cash for the release of Elmer and Grace. They are giving me two weeks to get the cash. The same woman will show up at the popcorn-packing building at noon on Sunday, June twelfth. It will take everything I have, but I am willing to give it all to them if they spare the lives of my friend and his wife."

Uncle Jay said, "What are you going to do, Henry?"

Henry was pacing like a lion on the prowl. "I don't know just yet, Jay. I turned the ransom note over to the Bureau of Investigation. I know for a fact that they have an open investigation on Verne Miller for a bank robbery near the Twin Cities, but they didn't seem to be interested in finding two Indians. Maybe the letter Alfred's mother wrote to him might stir up their interest, especially if it's connected to Verne Miller."

Bob said, "That is *exactly* what I told these boys. That letter is very valuable when it comes to finding Alfred's parents."

Henry turned to me. "Alfred, son, I think we need to get that letter to the Bureau of Investigation as soon as possible. You and your buddies stay clear of this situation and let the police handle it. I was young once, and I know you want to help, but these guys are dangerous, and the situation is way over your heads. It is organized crime and very deadly." He walked in front of us. "Promise me you will lie low and let us handle this."

I nodded in agreement, all the while thinking there was no chance I was going to put my parents' lives in his or anyone else's hands. I would find them before it was too late! And that was all there was to it!

Though I was thankful to Lucky for helping us get a job, I was also seeing another side of him that made me question his intentions. I wondered how far he would go to catch Verne Miller. Would he maybe even risk my life?

The work Orson, Junior, and I did was plenty enough. Not only did it cover our lodging and food, but we had extra cash. Since we worked on commission, a week of good attendance provided quite a stash. Junior was saving to help his grandmother; Orson, to help his father buy a car; and me, I really wanted an Indian motorcycle, but I decided I would help my father so he wouldn't have to leave us anymore to work in the cities.

But I had a feeling no amount of money would settle him down and cure the war ghosts he was running from.

Every spare minute I had, I used for training. Orson, Junior, and Willow had even started running with me for encouragement, but Willow was the only one who lasted and was still running with me. She was hanging around with us more and more. She was loads of fun. I liked the way she always made us laugh.

After my lunch breaks, I trained for the fight by jumping rope and sparring practice bouts with Bob.

Uncle Jay was staying with Henry over in the nice part of town. In the evenings he trained me hard, alternating between a heavy punching bag and a speed bag. He even had me shadowboxing with a mirror I borrowed from the acrobat team.

Word about my upcoming fight spread through the amusement park like gossip at the Saturday afternoon quilting parties my grandmother used to have. The whole darn carny clan cheered me on as I ran by. I felt like their sacrificial lamb being prepared for a grand offering.

The padded mitts Uncle Jay wore on his hands seemed to be improving my striking speed and combination punches.

Uncle Jay said, "I want you to fight like Jack Dempsey, explosive and aggressive."

"Be fair, Uncle," I said. "I don't even know who Dempsey is, but I do know who you are. Let's keep this simple."

Laughing, Uncle Jay said, "Sure, I can do that!"

Uncle Jay wanted me to crouch, bob, and weave, leaving as little of myself open as possible. He had me spar with a rapid sequence of blows and swift side movements. We practiced head movements, combination punching, and effective counterpunching, for a good defense.

At fifteen I was big for my age, but I was still going to be punching above my weight. Bob and Uncle Jay gave me extra meat to eat, and little by little I added some muscle weight.

The night before the fight, I lay in my bed unable to sleep. Time seemed to crawl by. The more anxious I got to catch some shut-eye, the more wide awake I became. I was as restless as the old cougar, Ned, that roamed Medicine Creek bottom.

Just as I dozed off, I heard, "Hey, Nephew! GET UP!"

I couldn't believe it was already Saturday, the morning of the big fight. The early dawn fog covering the path in front of me indicated it was going to be a scorcher today. Willow joined me from the stables. The five-mile jog along the river gave me ample time to figure things out. The eastern horizon was turning pale pink, a group of clouds spreading across the sky like a pair of open hands.

I pointed to the sky. "I am thankful that the Creator is giving us a sign that he is with us."

Still running next to me, Willow smiled with a thumbs-up.

The big night came much too soon.

Let the Thunder Begin

The fight tent, not too far from Fourth and Pearl, was busting at its seams from a sold-out crowd. I was directed to dress in a small side tent.

Bob said, "Son, let me wrap your hands with these cotton strips."

I opened my hands and held them out to him. Placing a loop over my thumb, he wrapped between my fingers and round and round my wrist.

He said, "You have some big paws for your age. I think it will be to your advantage tonight. This wrap under your gloves should protect your knuckles and wrists from fractures."

Uncle Jay said, "Okay, Nephew, let's get you laced up."

I fit my hands into a pair of dark brown leather boxing gloves Lucky had found somewhere. Uncle Jay laced them up, snug against my hands. The gloves felt good.

Lucky winked at me. "I know you are used to wearing five-ounce gloves, but the six ounces are the newest craze and will give you a better punch."

It was time! The big tent was packed to the hilt.

"Come on, son, let's do this!" said Uncle Jay. I followed him and Lucky toward the fight tent entrance.

A lone spotlight shone on the door, and Max Stolz danced by in front of us, adorned in a red silk robe with a colorful embroidered dragon on the back. Weaving and throwing punches in the air to the song "Puttin' On the Ritz" by Fred Astaire, Stolz laughed as he went by.

Several pretty girls followed Stolz toward the ring, holding number signs. The fight tent speakers blared over the deafening shouts of a cheering crowd and the mesmerizing display of colored lights.

"It's your turn, boy. Go in there and knock Stolz's socks off." Bob tried to sound confident, but I knew he and Uncle Jay were both about as nervous as I was. It was obvious we were against the odds.

The song "Piccolo Pete" by Ted Weems and his orchestra carried me into the big tent and toward the ring. I tried copying Max Stolz's dramatic entrance by dancing and swinging and punching at the empty air.

I recognized Lucky's voice in the crowd. "Go get 'em, Alfred!" I also knew he was only putting on a front and was hoping I would lose.

Orson, Junior, and Willow followed us in. Parading behind them were the prettiest hoochie-coochie girls adorned in the finest pizzazz the carnies could muster up. The crowd whistled and clapped at the girls. All the drama couldn't muffle all the laughter. I was sure it was at the robe I wore. A blue rabbit wearing red boxing gloves was painted on the back of Bob's blue robe. It read *Cohen the Fighting Hare*.

Stepping into the twenty-by-twenty-foot square called a ring, I took my corner. Uncle Jay put a stool down for me to sit on.

I sized up my opponent, Max Stolz. He looked deadly. He wasn't much bigger than me, but he was much stockier, with a thick muscular neck and shoulders. His blond hair didn't match his ruddy, scarred-up face. It was obvious that his nose had been broken far too many times. I thought, *I'm in for a heck of a fight.*

Uncle Jay, being my official trainer, was the only one moving in and out of my corner. I could see my friends Orson, Junior, and Willow seated ringside below me. They all gave me a victory wave. I was sure someone else waved at the back of the tent, but there were just too many people to make them out. I was nervous and probably seeing things that weren't there. Uncle Jay reminded my team to stay on the other side of the rope no matter what happened. I moved my attention back to where it needed to be, in the ring!

Uncle Jay said, "Nephew, remember to stay away from the ropes. You do not want to get backed up against them."

Bob handed Uncle Jay an empty metal coffee can for me to spit in. I took a knee and said a quick prayer.

As soon as I stood up, Uncle Jay pushed my mouthpiece in and nudged me forward. "You can do this, son. Go get him!"

The distinct voice of the fight announcer drowned out the squeal of the loudspeaker. "Ladies and gentlemen, welcome to the fight tent, right here in Sioux City, Iowa. Now, for all of you in attendance and for all those who wish they were here, let's get ready for thunnnnderrrr! The judges are seated in front and will keep scorecards on each fighter.

"Now, introducing the first fighter, in the red corner and wearing red, with a record of twenty-five wins, three losses, and one draw, let's give a big warm welcome to the acclaimed powerhouse, and a local boy, lightweight Max 'Powerhouse' Stolz, weighing in at one hundred and thirty-five pounds.

"Now, introducing the contender, in the blue corner and wearing blue, a newcomer on the scene, a young Native man all the way from Iron Nation, South Dakota, with the heart and guts of a wild bull elk. With no wins and no losses, fighting lightweight and weighing in at one hundred and thirty-five pounds, join me in welcoming Alfred 'Big Heart' Swallow to Sioux City's greatest attraction and our main event."

I was shocked. I'd weighed in as a feather-weight a few minutes ago at one hundred and twenty-six pounds. Now I'd magically moved up to a lightweight class to stage a fair fight with Stolz. I had a feeling Lucky had something to do with this, and it wasn't good.

The ring announcer said, "We will have twelve rounds with three-minute bouts and a maximum of forty-seven minutes overall. Any violation of the following rules will be considered a foul. The referee will give you a warning the first time, but a second-time foul will result in a point deduction, and the third time you can be disqualified." He looked directly at me. "Understand?"

I nodded that I did.

The announcer continued, "You cannot hit your opponent on the break, you cannot hit your opponent when he is down, and if you are knocked out of the ring, you have to the count of twenty to get back in unassisted. If you are floored, you have to the count of ten seconds to get back up on your feet, or it is considered a knockout. If you knock your opponent down, you must go to the opposite corner while the referee makes the count. Last, but not least, the referee can stop the fight at any time if he sees fit. *Understand?*"

I nodded again that I understood the boxing rules. I just wished to get this over with and go find my parents!

The announcer said, "Okay, fighters, touch gloves, and let the thunder begin!"

Cry Victory

Dancing from one foot to the next, I swerved from left to right, right to left. I was throwing my punches one after another, and most of them landed right where I wanted.

I met Stolz's punches with a variety of crisp, smooth moves. Keeping my lead hand stretched forward in front of my body, I held my other hand near my chin for protection.

The bell rang to signal the end of the first round. *Whew!*

I returned to my corner. Uncle Jay cooled me down with a wet towel.

Uncle Jay and Bob were talking at the same time. Uncle Jay said, "The first round has given us a good idea of Stolz's style, but also, he has an idea of how you fight as well. This next round he might move in for the knockout. Watch Stolz's left uppercut, his underhand close-up punch. It gets his opponents every time."

Bob said, "Use your jabs to set up your power punches and gauge your range. You need to distract Stolz. And most of all, remember, boxing is an art . . . dance, stay light on your feet, and have your arms ready to ward off punches. You can do this!"

Weaving and bobbing, I came out on the second round ready. I used my left-hand jab to set up a power punch with my right. But Stolz already had me figured out. He came at me like a raging bull, pounding me with his skilled punches inside his six-ounce horsehide gloves. I was outmatched. My left shin throbbed as my old injury flared up, and I went down. I hit the floor of the ring.

The referee leaned over to count me down with his fingers in the air. "One . . . two . . . three . . . four . . ."

I tried my best to get back up, but my legs were useless.

The crowd's booing was deafening. It was obvious I was the underdog here.

Uncle Jay shouted at me, "Get up, son! You can do this!"

The anger of thinking my parents had abandoned me, the anger of my grandfather leaving me when I needed him most, the anger at being beat at St. John's, and the anger at the cruel treatment and hate my people and I had to live with *all* released inside of me.

Somewhere in the booing I heard a familiar voice: "Go, Big Heart!"

I jumped up at the count of six, ready for more. Tucking my head down toward my shoulders, I charged my opponent like a buffalo bull in the fight of his life. I threw a cross punch, straight forward with my rear glove to block his vision. It worked. Stolz staggered back.

The bell rang, and the second round ended.

Uncle Jay doused me with water. Bob shouted, "You need to keep weaving and bobbing. Wear him out! You have the advantage in stamina, being lighter in weight. Again, stay away from his combinations!"

Even with all the swelling and sweat in my eyes, I could see her. It was Sage, standing in the back against the tent wall. It looked like her aunt, Mrs. Red Elk, was next to her. I knew if I'd ever had to win in my life, it was now.

I had something beyond the desire and drive to win this match. A spirit of victory. Victory for Sage, for my grandfather, for my parents, for me.

Time for round three, and I was ready! I hunched forward for protection and headed straight for Stolz. Bobbing and weaving, I alternated my hands, trying to get Stolz to overcommit.

I could hear Lucky barking through the fat cigar he clenched between his teeth, "Go with the punches. Don't try and fight him back. Just stay out of Stolz's way!"

I wasn't about to listen to Lucky, and I wasn't about to be his pawn anymore!

Stolz rabbit-punched me in the back of my head. Falling to my knees, I was surprised the referee or judges didn't catch that. My arms were getting heavy, most likely from the extra ounces added to my gloves.

As I danced toward Stolz, every bit of my training sparked through my memory. All my guilt, anger, shame, and pain fueled my desire to win. The fire raged deep; I was on top of my game this time.

Digging the back of my foot into the canvas, I changed the trajectory of my punches. Pacing my breath, I threw a straight punch with my left and followed with a hook from my right hand in a short side movement. It took Stolz by surprise. I had him on the ropes. Stolz went down on one knee. I stepped back, waiting for him to get up. He stood up and quickly regained his footing.

The disgruntled noise from the crowd was getting louder and louder. I kept my focus.

Stolz came at me, aiming for a knockout. He grazed my chin but failed to take me down. I came back with a one-two combination. I threw a jab and cross punch in succession and channeled all my strength through my upper body and into an uppercut that landed on Stolz's chin. He went down with a grunt.

I walked back to my corner. The referee counted down: *one . . . two . . . three . . . eight . . .*

It was final. Stolz was officially down in the third round. The crowd was on their feet.

The announcer made his way to the ring. "Ladies and gentlemen, we go to the judges' scorecards."

A low murmur spread through the tent. I could hear my heart beating in my head.

The announcer opened the scorecards. "By unanimous decision, all three judges score victory by knockout. Our winner and the new champion, Alfred 'Big Heart' Swallow."

I was spinning inside from the noise and excitement. The referee and the fight manager presented me with a gold championship belt and a brown envelope that I assumed was the purse, the money that I'd earned. I held the belt up for a photo shoot for the local newspaper.

"Hoka hey, Big Heart, you did it!" I barely heard my friends' victory cries over the booming voices from a surprised crowd and the commotion outside the tent. I watched Lucky move like a bullet toward the ruckus. I had a feeling that Verne Miller was on the run with a couple of G-men on his tail in hot pursuit.

After a few more handshakes and photos, I made my way toward my friends Orson, Junior, and Willow. I was craning my neck to get a glimpse of Sage. I felt a tap on my shoulder. I spun around so fast I almost knocked Sage over. She was with her aunt, Mrs. Red Elk.

Sage threw her arms around me. "Alfred, I was so worried about you, and I am so happy to see you alive. I'm so glad you won and didn't get beat up too much!"

Hugging her back, I laughed at how I must look: one swollen eye, a busted lip, and blood and snot smeared across my face. "Good to see you, Sage. I am glad I didn't get too beat up either. He-he." I could tell Sage was just as excited to see me as I was to see her. I nodded to Mrs. Red Elk. "It's good to see you too. I missed all of you and thought a couple of times this past winter I would never see you again. But here we are."

Mrs. Red Elk said, "We heard you ran away from the Catholic Indian school in Chamberlain. I know that school. It has problems. I am glad you are alive and well. I promised Sage that when we came to Sioux Falls to visit my brother, we would drive to Sioux City and look for you. Then Sage saw your name on a postcard pinned up at the corner drug store, the one on the corner of Dakota and Coteau Streets in Pierre."

"Of course! I remember the store."

Mrs. Red Elk smiled big. "That settled it! I moved my trip to see my brother up, and here we are! Alfred, it is time to check into the boarding house we are staying at, but we will be back. We plan to be here around three to four days."

Sage winked at me. "See you tomorrow, Alfred Big Heart. You have always been a winner in my book."

I choked on my words. "See you both tomorrow."

Sage felt me watching her. She turned around and waved. My heart did a flip-flop.

Fame was short-lived! Lucky showed up. "You put up a good fight, Alfred. Sorry I couldn't tell you more about the operation. Although winning wasn't part of the bureau's plan, deep down I wanted you to win and take that belt away from that arrogant Stolz. And by golly! You did it! Sure enough, Verne Miller was here, but he slipped right through our fingers. But we have an idea where he might be headed."

I thought, *Good! I wish you could have put that effort into locating my parents.*

Lucky said, "Jack wants to see you. He said he'd be waiting."

I knew I would have to explain everything, including my age. I dreaded seeing Jack.

I handed Bob his lucky rabbit robe and gloves, then said to him and Uncle Jay, "Thank you both for your expertise and training. I couldn't have won this fight without you. Now we can put all our efforts into looking for my parents."

They both nodded in agreement.

I said, "I will see you both tomorrow. I need to go see what Jack wants."

Bob said, "Don't be surprised if you see me later."

I wondered what he meant and was going to ask him when Willow said, "Alfred, that was quite a fight. I am so proud of you. It's time for me to go back to the stables and call it a night. I will check in with you tomorrow."

I could tell Uncle Jay was impressed with Willow by the way he was watching her.

Orson and Junior accompanied me to Jack's tent. He hollered through the open tent door, "Come in, Alfred!"

I sheepishly walked in and took a seat. I didn't waste a minute. "I don't blame you for being mad, because I outright lied to you. I'm fifteen and not eighteen, and—"

"Enough, young man. I called you in to congratulate you. I am thrilled you kicked old arrogant Stolz's hind end. It was long overdue. As for lying to me, you must remember you can never fool a carny. I knew how old you and your friends were from day one.

"I called you in to let you know we are celebrating your big win tonight! And you and your friends are our guests of honor. The party is at the midway where all the music and lights are!"

Last of Her Kind

Bob called to us from his tent, "Good timing, boys! Come over here and hold this gunnysack open for me."

A strange feeling came over me. I wasn't listening to one word Bob was saying. Instead, I was staring at the picture on the gunnysack he was holding open. A movement from my medicine bundle under my shirt was a sign to pay attention. I looked around the room, but for the life of me I just couldn't see anything unusual. Then there it was! A picture of a steamboat on the side of the gunnysack, with the name SS *Emerson Ferry & Packard Co.* stamped in cursive above the steamboat. Yes! That was it! I was certain that my parents were being held prisoner by Fritz and Verne somewhere on the *Emerson Ferry & Packard* steamboat. Wherever that was.

It took a while to explain my insight to Bob, Orson, and Junior. Orson and Junior understood my medicine and my intuition, but Bob was amused and skeptical.

Laughing like a wild hyena, Bob said, "I know you are sincere, Alfred, but you want me to believe that an invisible messenger is going to crack a case that some of the best lawmen can't." He took his apron off. "But I'll go along with your so-called gut feeling just to please you. We can head over to the *Emerson* first thing in the morning. She's docked up on the Missouri River not too far from here. We'll have to drive over in my truck. I'll show you there's nobody on board. Been docked there for the past three months."

Bob smiled a lopsided grin. "But for now, we are going to make the most of Jack's freebies. I'm sure he'll be pourin' some of Sioux City's finest corn liquor. Hard to get hooch like that with all that darn prohibition going on. Makes my mouth water just thinking about it."

Bob was right. Jack didn't hold back a thing. A stunning display of colored lights set a festive mood. Red Nichols's "I Got Rhythm" blasted out on a crackling loudspeaker. The party was on!

"Wow, this is remarkable," I said to Orson and Junior.

"Yup, never seen anything like it before," said Orson.

Carnies young and old, tall and short, fat and skinny, and everything in between were dancing, laughing, and feasting in celebration of my victory.

The bearded lady saw us and instantly made a beeline for Junior. All three of us said, *"Oh no!"*

She grabbed Junior by the arm and said, "Come on, son, let's dance."

She whizzed Junior into the center of the dance area. Orson and I craned our necks to see the spectacle.

I said to Orson, "I think I have more rhythm in my little finger than Junior has in his entire body. He is as stiff as a day-old dead squirrel."

The crowd clapped and egged them on. Junior shot us a mean look that said, "Don't you dare laugh."

Oh, but we did. In fact, we darned near split a gut laughing. It was priceless.

We didn't say one word to Junior when he returned, but he knew we had a good story on him to tell our friends back home.

I yawned and said to Orson and Junior, "Not to be a killjoy, but I think we need to turn in for the night. We have important business to tend to in the morning."

Carny mornings always came on lazy and slow, since most carnies worked late long after the crowd thinned out. We were on our way to Bob's tent. Willow was waving at us.

"Hey, guys! Where you off to?" I recognized the voice and spun around. It was Sage.

I thought, *Okay, first Willow, now Sage. Will we ever get this show on the road?*

I said, "Why'd you come so early? I mean, where's your aunt?"

Sage said, "She dropped me off. She will come back for me around three thirty. She wanted me to spend some time with you and maybe convince you all to go with us back to Pierre."

No chance of that until I find my parents, I thought.

I said, "That's great, Sage! We have something to do that is important. I guess you will have to come along with us."

Sage said with her hands on her hips, "I guess that settles it. I'm going along with you, so you might as well give me the scoop!"

While we waited for Bob to come around, I introduced Sage to Willow. By their chatter, I could tell they'd taken a liking to one another.

It was time to fill Sage and Willow in on all the details surrounding my parents' disappearance. They listened, and by the time I finished, Bob showed up with bloodshot eyes and a guilty grin.

He said, "Whoa . . . where'd these pretty little ladies show up from? I reckon they are coming along with us, right? Hope I have enough room in my truck."

I said, "Don't worry, we can ride in the truck bed."

It was midmorning when we reached the abandoned steamboat.

I whispered, "Hey, guys, here is an ideal lookout tucked in the crook of this dead tree. We have an excellent view of the boat."

The *Emerson* was the last of her kind: a long, flat steamboat that was maybe around one hundred and sixty-two feet long. She was nestled up against the shore with her bow pointing upstream. A ramp ran close to the water level from her deck to the shore.

It looked like she had a main deck at the bottom level, and a boiler deck on the next level. I could make out a row of windows and doors on the boiler deck. I assumed they were cabins.

I craned my neck so I could get a better view. At the very top was the pilot house, where there were several glass windows. I was sure it was where Henry Emerson steered his boat. Two large smokestacks towered nearby. At the rear was a stern wheel that propelled the steamboat forward. Dark chunks of coal were stacked on the deck next to the engine room for the fire needed to move the boat.

At the front of the boat was a flagstaff with a tattered and faded blue flag whipping in the wind. On the flag was the image of a steamboat and the words *SS Emerson Ferry & Packard Co*.

I said, "This is it! I know it! This is where Fritz and Verne have my parents. I just pray they are still alive!"

Gangsters on the Run

Bob said, "I really doubt they are here. But like I said earlier, that old steamboat has been boarded up for a few months, and I am certain there is not a soul on board, so I think we should just walk on up and look around."

I knew Bob thought spirit helpers and dreams were a bunch of hogwash. Maybe I needed to prove him wrong.

Bob said, "Well, let's get moving." We followed him on board.

Orson and Junior went toward the main deck. Bob climbed up to the hurricane deck to check out the pilot house. Sage, Willow, and I started for the cabins on the boiler deck. We had just stepped out of one of the vacant cabins when I spotted a car pulling up to the dock.

It was a black Cadillac Town Sedan. Two men stepped out of the car and started toward the boat. One of the men was carrying a short, wide duffel bag, and the other man had a long, narrow bag. Both were dressed in pinstriped suits, with colorful ties, and wore Fedora felt hats, just like the picture I had seen of the crime boss Al Capone in Mrs. Red Elk's magazine.

For their own sake, I was hoping Bob, Orson, and Junior saw the visitors too. I had a sinking feeling it was the same car that had delivered the ransom note to Henry Emerson.

Creeeeak. The cabin door next to us opened. I pushed Sage and Willow back into the shadows.

The men disappeared inside the cabin. Within minutes, a tall man wearing a suit and hat took a seat outside the cabin on the left side of the doorway. He was holding a tommy gun. A woman came out. She paced the dock smoking a cigarette. Somehow, I knew that they knew we were nearby.

Sage whispered, "Look . . . near the trees on the road . . ."

A truck silently rolled into a very well-hidden tree line. Two men got out and disappeared into the trees closest to the *Emerson.*

I whispered, "That truck looks like Uncle Jay's."

The man and woman went back inside the cabin. I said, "Now! It's our chance. Let's go! Follow me!"

We made it down to the main deck.

"Psst!" It was Junior and Orson. They motioned us over to join them by the coal pile. They had a good view of the cabin door through a hole in the deck above.

I said, "I think it's the same woman that delivered the ransom note to Henry."

The man came back out. This time he had a beer in his hands. He resumed his guard. We continued to watch the man, unaware that as we watched him, someone was watching us.

Junior said, "Hey, I hear something . . ."

Everything went black, and my breath caught in a scratchy hood forced over my head. From the muffled noises around me, I was sure my friends were in the same predicament. I could make out several distinct voices. I assumed there were at least two to four gangsters on us.

"Hey, Verne, looks like we have us some spies, eh?" a deep voice said.

I heard Sage say, "Let us go!"

At the sound of Sage's voice, I struggled to free myself. A kick in my side made my breath catch in the pit of my gut. "Aaaagh!" I yelled.

Another voice said, "Shut up, kid! Hey! I recognize you from the fight last night. You are Elmer Swallow's kid. This is 'bout as good as catching me a Missouri River paddlefish. Got the old man, his woman, and now his kid. Fritz is going to like this a whole lot!"

The man with the deep voice commanded, "All of you! Get up on your feet! Now!"

Someone pushed a hard object between my shoulder blades. I assumed it was a pistol. The person holding it said, "Get moving! *Now!*"

With each step I took, the muffled voices ahead of me grew louder and clearer. A door creaked open, and with one push, my captor sent me tumbling forward onto the floor with my friends on top of me.

I whispered, "Are you all okay?"

Sage, Willow, Orson, and Junior whispered back, "Yeah." I felt better knowing we were all together and still alive. At least for now.

A faint voice said, "Leave him alone. It's me you want. Don't hurt my boy."

"Father? Is that you?" I shouted. I recognized my father's voice, and he sounded hurt.

With a kick to my side, the pistol man said, "Shut your trap, kid! No talking! YOU HEAR?"

A hand felt its way down my arm until it found my hand and held on tight. It was my mother's hand. I had sworn I'd never cry again, but here I was with tears rolling down my cheeks.

My mother softly whispered, "I am sorry your father and I put you and your friends in harm's way." She quickly pulled her hand away. "Someone is coming. Just stay quiet, and they might leave you alone."

Bump . . . *BANG! BUMP.* Something hit the wall of the cabin with a loud thud. Mother pushed my head down. I felt around for Sage. *Too late.* Thousands of fine shards from breaking glass sprayed through the room.

Zip! POP! The whistle of bullets filled the air. Judging by the whizzing sounds, the gun fight was close by on the deck.

My jaw clenched at the painful scream coming from one of the gangsters: "I'm hit! I'm going down!" I could only imagine what the thud followed by a gurgling sound was.

A voice that sounded like the pistol man shouted, "Rush them! Don't let them get away!"

Another voice I didn't recognize shouted, "Aaaagh . . . waaah! They're packing! Take cover!"

Even with my loud and heavy breathing inside the hood over my head, I could hear the rapid pop of gunfire and the agony in the grunts around me. My stomach heaved with fear. My mother held my hand tight. I held hers back.

Another cry: "HELP ME! Help me . . ." One loud thud, and all was silent. I faintly detected a sickly sweet and metallic smell. It was the smell of blood.

"Henry! Quick, get those hoods off and untie them."

I couldn't believe it! It was the voice of Uncle Jay.

It dawned on me! The two men who had walked to the trees from Uncle Jay's truck . . . It was Uncle Jay and Henry Emerson.

Bob appeared next to Uncle Jay and winked at me. "I'll be doggone. Made a believer out of me."

Real Water,
Real Me

Orson, Junior, Sage, Willow, and I sucked in as much fresh air as we could. I could taste it, and it was wonderful!

My parents were weak but able to stand and walk.

I said, "Mother, are you okay? Father, what about you?"

My parents answered, "We are okay. We just need some nourishment."

We followed Uncle Jay, Emerson, and Bob across the ramp to the riverbank. The whining sound of sirens and flashing red lights from five black Ford Model A police cars and a black-and-white paddy wagon sped down the road toward the *Emerson*.

Squinting against the intense sunrays reflecting off the water, I could make out two men stepping out of the first car. One of the men looked like it might be Lucky. Three more men climbed out of the second car. I assumed that, like Lucky, they were officers from the Bureau of Investigation.

They were almost to us when a fellow officer shouted across the ramp to them, "We got Fritz, but Verne Miller got away! He's in the trees. We need help to try and flush him out!"

They all left in hot pursuit on foot and in their vehicles.

Bob said, "I have a strange feeling that Verne Miller is long gone by now."

Uncle Jay said, "I'm sure, like with any addiction, it will only be a matter of time before he gets the urge to rob another bank and his luck runs out."

Finally standing solid on the bank, I said to my friends, "Thank you for helping me find my parents. I'm so glad you are all safe. I would have never forgiven myself if any of you were hurt."

It was my mother's hug that broke me. I felt like I was two years old again and needed my mother to tell me everything was going to be okay. I couldn't stop the wet stream of emotion that flowed down my cheeks. I knew my friends were watching, but I just couldn't help it.

My father dried his eyes on his shirtsleeve. "Son, we knew you would come, because your mother prayed for you to find us. I prayed you wouldn't get hurt once you got here. We need to gather our things before we return to Iron Nation."

Hearing my father say those words was music to my ears. I was glad he was going to come back home to Iron Nation.

My voice was broken, but my words were true. "You both have no idea what we endured, and maybe you never will. Grandfather has left us, and Elmer is very sick." My mother wept softly as I continued, "Please come home and bring our family back together again. We need you."

Mother said, "Son, we are so sorry. Things will get better. I promise you."

The sun was setting in the western sky, a blazing yellow ball hanging low in orangish-pink clouds. Henry said, "What a day! Everyone can meet up at my house for some good food and plan-making business."

"I think that is an excellent idea. Let's go!" Uncle Jay answered.

I said to my parents, "I am going with my friends to the amusement park a few miles north past the railroad hub. When you're finished up with your plans, you know where to find us. Besides, I have to say goodbye to Goldie."

Orson, Junior, and I sat on one side of Bob's pickup box, while Willow and Sage sat on the other side. Bob bounced us over the ruts in the river road. We talked and laughed until our sides ached.

Orson and Junior went with Bob to help him unload a barrel of popcorn. I walked with Sage and Willow to the stables.

I said, "I sure am going to miss Goldie."

Willow said, "I am sure you will, and I am sure she will miss you too."

Sage said to Willow, "I am going to be a veterinarian when I finish school."

Willow said, "That's a good occupation if you love animals. Me, I love horses. I taught myself about horses, or should I say, they taught me!"

We laughed, because we all understood the sheer determination a horse can muster up.

We spent the evening saying our goodbyes to our carny friends and collecting our pay from Jack.

I said, "Let's meet at the amusement park entrance tomorrow morning."

Everyone agreed.

Mrs. Red Elk came for Sage to go back to the boarding house for the night. Me, I sat with Goldie until way past dark.

The morning sky was growing lighter and brighter by the minute. Everyone showed up at the front entrance gate at the same time. Emerson was riding with my parents in my mother's black Model A, Bob was in his truck, and Uncle Jay was in his truck with the wooden buckboards. Even

Sage and Mrs. Red Elk showed up. Everyone was there except Willow, and I was disappointed. We stood around wearing smiles and leaning on truck fenders, drinking cream soda.

Henry said, "Hey, boys, looks like my old steamer will be making a trip upriver after all. It didn't take much to get her fired up this morning. I had to replace a couple of parts on the furnace, but she is good to go. I decided to make a final run and deliver a load of pipe up to Fort Pierre and bring a couple of farm implements back.

"I would like to stop over at Iron Nation and talk with your superintendent. I think if he sees we have enough money and political support to maintain a school, he will let Iron Nation Day School reopen next fall."

Mrs. Red Elk let out a squeal. "That would be absolutely wonderful!"

Henry went on, "Elmer and Grace and Jay are driving back west to Iron Nation. I offered to let you boys ride with me to Iron Nation. You can be a big help to Bob and me."

A familiar neigh caught me off guard. It was Willow and Goldie.

I said, "I was hoping you'd show up. I wanted to introduce you to my uncle Jay."

Willow's brown face blushed. She smiled. "Hi, Jay. I'm Willow."

Uncle Jay was just as shy. "Hi, I'm Jay." He reached out to shake Willow's hand just as she reached out to shake his. They jammed fingers. "Ouch!"

Everyone roared with laughter.

Willow said, "I have a surprise for you, Alfred. The carny family decided that Goldie belongs with you if you want her and can afford to feed her. With a drought and all, hay is hard to get. The carnies said Goldie won't be any good without you. So, here she is. I guess you will need to figure out how to get her home."

Piping up, Henry said, "That's an easy fix. She can ride with Alfred and his friends on the *Emerson* all the way to Iron Nation, to her new home."

Goldie whinnied like she understood, which I was sure she did.

After talking to her aunt, Sage said, "Alfred, is it okay if I ride back to Iron Nation with you, Orson, and Junior on the *Emerson*?"

I practically screamed with joy. "Yes! Of course it's okay!"

Father and Uncle Jay smudged the *Emerson* of any bad memories.

Willow gave me a hug. "Alfred, I never told you that you remind me of my little brother. His name was Troy Lightning Bow, and he died in Chilocco Indian School from scarlet fever. I am going to miss you. Don't be surprised if I show up someday in Iron Nation."

Willow gave me a big hug and smile and walked away with Uncle Jay toward his truck.

By high noon, we were chugging up the Missouri River toward home. Goldie was settled comfortably in a storage compartment turned horse stall on the main deck. She had plenty of hay and water and a shovel just for me, to keep her stall clean.

Sage, Orson, Junior, and I sat near the bow. We watched the big muddy river twist and churn below.

I said to them, "I believe something happened to me during our river run. I got to know the real me inside."

Orson and Junior looked confused, but Sage knew exactly what I meant.

I said, "I mean, I always thought there was something wrong with me. I was running from spirits and people like James O'Neil, Johnny Krugerbery, Joe Harvey, Fritz Emerson, Verne Miller, and at one time, even you, Junior."

Junior looked at me. His droopy eyes didn't even blink.

I continued, "So much emotional running made me cynical and bitter many times. Even the time I hurt my legs in a wolf attack or the time I

almost got one cut off, I still didn't wake up to see
the truth about myself. At this moment, my eyes
are wide open, and I know that I can trust others."

Orson yawned. "I am glad you finally see and
accept your flaws, old buddy. You don't know how
many times I came *real* close to boxing you silly
because you were so darn stubborn . . ." His voice
faded off.

I said, "Orson, Junior, and Sage, you are my
best friends. I almost forgot our friend Elizabeth.
I vow to always be there for you four, and I am
sure you will be there for me. Right?"

No answer, because Orson and Junior were
snoozing in the warm sun. Obviously lulled to sleep
by the gentle rocking motion, they hadn't heard
a word of my vow.

Sage chuckled. "I'm still listening, and I agree."

Sage listened as I reflected on my life and my
time with my grandfather, on his sacred stories
about water, on protecting the Missouri River,
and on my vision of the five giant beavers and the
huge dams they would build in the future that
would forever change the river's course.

I said, "I now know that I am Big Heart, a
name given to me from the Thunder Beings. I have
learned to trust others. I have learned to accept
my grieving, my losses, and my limitations. Life
is now real for me, and when we are real, we are

not afraid of being hurt, because in the end, life is worth it."

Sage nodded with a gentle smile.

I couldn't wait to get home to Elmer; my grandmother; my community and extended family; and my animals, Blue Boy, Anpo, and especially my beloved dog, Chepa. And now, I'd be introducing my new edition, Goldie. I could only imagine Blue Boy's surprise.

A golden eagle swooped down and followed us for a mile, soaring with the air currents coming off the river. I didn't know what the future held for me, but I did know that I was ready to face the world.

The Pick-Sloan Act and the Five Giant Beavers

The Lower Brule Lakota people (Kul Wicasa Oyate) suffered when the United States government passed the Pick-Sloan Act in 1944. The act authorized the construction of five of the world's largest earthen dams across the main stem of the Missouri River in North Dakota and South Dakota. The magnitude of these structures challenged the imagination.

The Pick-Sloan Act inflicted devastation on five Sioux reservations: Standing Rock, Cheyenne River, Crow Creek, Yankton, and Lower Brule. The Pick-Sloan Act flooded the bottomland of the Missouri River Valley, destroying the entire town of Lower Brule, including the community of Iron Nation. Families were forced from their homes to barren upland regions. Miles of roads, houses, farms, ranches, and many sacred sites were flooded and demolished. Medicinal and food plants that had always sustained the people were lost forever.

Entire cemeteries of ancestors were uprooted and moved to higher ground.

Big Heart, near death at ninety-four years, remarked that the Pick-Sloan Act was the most devastating undertaking by the United States government ever against any tribe. The monumental impact is beyond measure.

lfreda Beartrack-Algeo is a storyteller and poet as well as an artist and illustrator. She is a member of the Lower Brule Lakota Nation, Kul Wicasa Oyate, Lower Brule, South Dakota, where she grew up surrounded by her extended family, her circle of family and friends. Alfreda uses various art forms to tell her stories. Alfreda says, "It is a very sensitive and beautiful experience to be a storyteller. There is a story in everything I create, from the smallest rock to the mightiest mountain. With every character born, every story shared, I add a piece of my spirit to this great matrix of life. As long as I have a story left to tell, I feel I have a responsibility to gift that story forward." Alfreda currently lives in beautiful Palisade, Colorado, with her spouse, David Algeo.

THE LEGEND OF BIG HEART
BOOKS 1 AND 2

The Land Grab • The Legend of Big Heart—Book 1 • 978-1-939053-40-4 • $9.95

The Roan Stallion • The Legend of Big Heart—Book 2 • 978-1-939053-48-0 • $9.95